i

Donald G. Parent

Book 1
The Lézard Family Chronicles
The Adventures of Lazarus Lézard
In
Lizard in a Blizzard

Art and Story by
Don Parent
With
Design and Digitization by:
Hailey Parent Buccarelli

Donald G. Parent

Welcome to another adventure from the wide-ranging mind of Donald G. Parent Jr: Publisher, Writer, Cartoonist, Musician/Songwriter, and Internet Pioneer.

Don is a 100% Disabled Vietnam Veteran.

Fiction, Fantasies, Cartoon Books, and Cartoon Strips:
The Lézard Family Chronicles:

- The Adventures of Lazarus Lézard in "Lizard in a Blizzard"
- The Adventures of Lorenzo Lézard - The Spy With One Thousand Faces

The Adventures of Professor A. Pismo Clam:
"Winning the Boston Marathon",

- Any Sea Horse Will Do",
- "Pismo's Surprise Party"
- and more

Publishing:

- First Internet Sports Fishing Magazine in the world: WWW.AllcoastSportfishing.Com
- WWW.Clam-Corp.Com

Non-Fiction Works:

- The Warzone PTSD Survivors Guide - 1st and 2nd Editions (3rd Edition available in 2016)
- WWW.PTSDHotline.Com
- WWW.VeteransHealthBlog.Com

Acknowledgements
And Notes:

- First and Foremost I want to thank my wife for almost 50 years Ginger Parent. She is my best friend now and forever!!! We married on my R and R Leave from Vietnam in 1967
- Hailey Parent is not only my first granddaughter, but she is also a fabulous artist. She took all my drawings, including the cover art, digitized it, and reworked them to my specifications and nitpicky expectations.
- Leah Parent Buccarelli (Hailey's mom) and Giovanni Buccarelli
- Kari Hassey (2nd daughter) and her husband Joe Hassey with our two granddaughters Hensley and Raelynn.
- I also wish to thank the whole Buccarelli family for adopting Hailey both lovingly and legally into their extended family. They have been wonderful to Hailey Parent Buccarelli.
- Thanks for some of the earlier art digitization go to Shea Dyke.
- Book layout: Thomas Harwick
(WWW.harwickt.wix.com/authorthomasharwick)
- Cover design: Jerry Dorris
WWW.Authorsupport.Com
- Editing by my beautiful niece, Marie Huntsinger
- A special thank you to my Mom Marilyn Parent, who is a special artist and gave me some of my earliest inspiration to do fun projects like this book. She, my sister Marcia and her husband Thor Helton have taken my mom's art to a whole new

level. Check it out:
http://northernreexposure.com/

Some of the fictional characters in this book are named after very old friends of mine:

- Keith Harriman - Can't forget his wife our good friend, Diana Harriman
- Allen Derby - Also will never forget his wife, Kathy Derby
- John Paul (Frenchie) LeBlanc
- A very special remembrance goes out to my friend who died next to me in the Vietnam War in 1968 - Lonny Lebombard. You will find a character named after him in the last third of this adventure.

All these above are special people in my life that have helped mold much of my thinking over the years.

Preface
Historical Fiction?

Although this is a work of fiction many of the characters, in this book, are actual historical men and women.

Also, most of the places, dates, and events in this novel are historically accurate.

There is a lot of interaction between real people from history, and fictional characters, and fictionalized events.

I back up all the Real People, Places, and Things with Endnotes in each chapter.

Being a research junkie made the writing of this book more fun than I have had with any other writing project I have done in the past.

HMS Queen Mary

Even the Ghost Story that takes place on the Queen Mary is drawn from sightings of a historic ghost. The Queen Mary has over 150 known ghosts haunting its decks. It is one of the most haunted places in the world. This book is not a ghost story; however there is one in it. My wife and I spent several nights on that magnificent ship, which was turned into a floating hotel. If you do not believe in ghosts now, a few nights stay may change your mind!

While writing this book, I attempted to cover ethical issues and the harm caused by prejudice in a way that younger and older readers will appreciate.

Having so much historical accuracy should make this story of interest to all age groups:

I hope you enjoy it as much as I enjoyed writing it. That being said I am now going to head out into the Mojave Desert of Southern California, where I live, to commune with some of my favorite talking lizards!!!

Thank You.

Don Parent

Donald G. Parent

Contents

Endnotes

Important Adventures in History:

*Endnotes:** At the end of each chapter you will find interesting facts. Watch for people, places, and things preceded by an *asterisk** in each chapter.

Adventures in Learning: Don't jump over these Endnotes. Being tied to this rollicking adventure they are a fun way to receive a history lesson.

Learn about Billy the Kid, Pat Garrett, and the Lincoln County War. Find out about Klondike Kate and Dawson City during the Gold Fever of the Nineteenth Century and much more.

Chapter 1
Travel Pains

Lazarus Lézard was feeling every day of his 80 Plus years on the planet earth. Traveling, while still exciting, was much easier on a body younger than he now walked in. The body he was dealing with today was more suited to an easy chair. It was ironic how the brain aged and matured like a fine wine while the body reversed itself toward infancy.

Thinking about this made him laugh. The idea of his green scaly butt in an oversize senior citizen diaper tickled him immensely.

The travel from his office in the Far Frozen North Country, to Europe involved many modes of transportation. Some of them, like the dog sledding leg across the snow-bound *Yukon, could be brutal on his old bones.

The last big dust-up caused by the Alaskan Miners digging for gold on Inuit Indian lands had been just too much for him. The search for gold and silver brought out the worst in people. The Inuit tribes had asked him to stand up for their rights, but the human miners would take little input from a grizzled old lizard, even one with his well-deserved reputation.

His years of good works in the frozen north were hard won. He would not let money crazed newcomers destroy the life that the Indians had built there over thousands of years.

The miners all carried rifles and sidearms. Their dreams of the next big gold strike danced around in their heads. This gave their trigger fingers spasms and made for a potential disaster.

His last few months of intervention had just barely pushed the miners back off Indian land. A tenuous peace was in place. For how long was anyone's guess.

He needed to get away from all the conflict for a while. He was ready for this trip into warmer climates and cooler heads. It sounded wonderful to him. He was glad the trip was finally underway.

Spending a few weeks in Paris with his egg brother Lorenzo would be a great interlude. After that, it was on to the United States to spoil the heck out of his grandkids.

Paris, France:

As always his time with Lorenzo was an extremely interesting interlude. Lorenzo had a way of turning everything into a special event. His life had been full of surprises that translated into many scales raising tales of adventure. Lazarus had enough of his problems for a while. He could escape his troubles and bury himself into his brother's stories.

Laz never tired of hearing his brother's tales of travels into the back streets of suspense and intrigue. In his younger years, he had been known as Lorenzo Lézard - "The Spy with a Thousand Faces."

He had spent many years in the ghettos and dark alleys as Europe's most famous war correspondent. While going undercover to get the hottest stories he had come to the attention of Europe's Spymasters. They had recruited him to keep his eyes peeled for plots against France, England, and the Western Free World.

His expertise with disguises and dialects allowed him to disappear into the guise of a Japanese street vendor, a Polish sausage maker, even a tambourine shaking Gypsy.

In their younger years, Lorenzo and Lazarus had been partially raised by world famous clown, and all around circus performer, Petit Pierre LeBow.

Lorenzo had learned all the performing tricks of the trade, including the art of makeup and much more from Pierre. The boys had even spent some school vacations traveling with Pierre to circuses around the East Coast of the United States.

Retelling the old stories would keep them up late reliving scenes from exotic nights sipping tea and eating dates on the *Kasbah to Champaign and caviar along the Rhine River in Germany.

Lorenzo talked about the times he almost froze his tail off on stake-outs below the onion-domed Cathedrals of Soviet Russia. He had nearly died of hunger and thirst crawling across the sand dunes of the Sahara.

His years of fighting against the German War Machine alone could fill a hundred books with stories of narrow escapes from the clutches of his brutal enemies. World War One had been a terrible period that shook the foundations of life on the whole planet.

Spending time with Lorenzo was exhilarating and exhausting all at the same time. He still had boundless energy and loved to take Lazarus to his favorite restaurants and bistros. He was well known in all of them. These daily adventures stretched into the wee hours of the night. Sometimes they fell into bed just as the stars began to blink out from the light of the rising sun.

Far too soon it was time to bid adieu to Lorenzo and "Gay Paree". Laz was off to visit his other family members in the United States. His brother called in a favor and got him on a military flight to Southampton, England just in time for his Atlantic Sea Voyage aboard The Queen Mary.

WWII was over, and it was now safe to travel the oceans again. Well, safe from marauding ships of war. Lazarus was soon to find that he wasn't immune from the things that could go bump in the night!!!

The Queen Mary:
His time aboard the Queen Mary from Southampton, England to New York gave Laz six days to recharge his batteries. The sea air and mild summer breezes were just what he needed to put a nice green hue back into his snout. He always found it hilarious that ocean travel could turn some human passengers green as well. Of course, this was not in a particularly attractive way. The sounds they made as they hung over the rail reminded him, in a real guttural way, of the miners on their hands and knees scrambling and grubbing for the little globs of yellow gold back home in the Yukon.

He had to shake his snout back and forth to push those ugly thoughts back down where they belonged. During his life, he had fought hard to see both sides of the issues. The miners could be hard to warm up to, but he still needed to understand their side as well.

He needed this trip. He couldn't keep his work problems from creeping in on him at the strangest times.

The Queen Mary: *Haunted Ship?

Speaking of strange things creeping around in his head, Lazarus was fascinated by the stories that were circulating regarding the ship he was sailing on, and the ghosts that could be walking its decks.

During the war, the *Queen Mary had been used for military operations such as troop transports. She made many voyages as a troop ship delivering soldiers from New York to Great Britain, Italy, and anywhere they were needed.

Because of the war, there were some horrible accidents that resulted in great loss of life.

In October 1942, the ship had an accident with one of her escort ships. She sliced through the light cruiser HMS Curacao causing the drowning of 239 sailors.

Lazarus heard some passengers saying they could hear screams and loud grinding metal sounds through the hull in the middle of the night.

During the day, it was easy to dismiss these stories as the musings of bored people with too much time on their hands.

But as the sun went down he had the feeling that strange things were going on just outside of his peripheral vision. He would turn rapidly seeing something just wiggle out of the corner of his eye.

Through his work and travels, he had seen many things that would have shocked and frightened most people. However, these fleeting feelings were still unnerving. It was as if something or someone was playing a game with him. It fascinated him!

One twilight evening, as he was walking down a hallway, he felt a cold, damp presence stalk straight through his body. This event stopped him in his tracks. Whatever it was, left his shirt dripping wet both in front and back. It was an experience that he would remember for years. Due to his many unique adventures, this didn't so much scare him as it gave him something bizarre to ponder.

He spent days quizzing crew members and searching the hallways hoping to re-experience this phenomenon. Spending years with Inuit's and the Indians of the Western United States had opened his mind to many legends and spiritual rituals. He was more intrigued than frightened. However, his fellow passengers didn't share his interest in quite the same way.

The crew had many stories of sightings and sounds that they couldn't explain away. Lazarus loved the mystery of situations like this, and it gave him hours of a lizard's version of Goosebumps during the remainder of the trip.

One evening, as darkness fell, Lazarus heard a loud commotion and jumped out of the way as crewmen ran anxiously past him toward the ruckus.

A group of adults was yelling and waving their hands in the air. Some children were missing, and all the parents were frantic. They had been looking for their kids for quite some time, and the search was made harder by a cloying mist that had begun to envelop the ship. Having a fog horn blow every so often was shredding their nerves to the bone.

The crew organized several search parties, and they split up into sections of the upper decks.

As the minutes stretched into hours, a deep fear began to overtake the groups. Whispers of evil doings began to circulate among the passengers. The creepy stillness of the night and the damp chilling fog did nothing to ease the unrest.

Everyone was jumpy, and people screamed at the slightest touch of someone's elbow or jumped out of their skin when one crew member accidentally dropped his flashlight.

Lazarus kept hearing an odd sound. He could swear he heard a little girl's voice whispering *"Come and join the party"*! It gave him the creeps, but he shook it off thinking his imagination was getting the better of him just like the others.

The search of the upper decks found no missing children. The parents were apoplectic by now. The fathers were cursing and yelling at everyone and everything. The mothers were broken down in tears and ripping at their clothes, dreading something awful must have happened.

The groups of searchers headed down into the bowels of the ship. The close quarters and darkness did nothing to relieve the bad feelings radiating through the thick oily air caused by the ship's engines.

As they walked deeper into the shadows they saw signs stating:

The deeper Lazarus climbed down into the ship, the louder the whispered; *"Come and join the party"* message entered his brain.

Over his years, he had experienced many frightening events but fearing for the safety of youngsters was always the hardest of them all to handle.

A woman next to him cried "Did you hear that"! Lazarus asked her what she meant. The woman had an odd look on her face and said, "I thought I heard a little girl say, '*Come and join the party*'! It gave me the willies"!

This invitation was not a coincidence, and it scared Lazarus down to the tips of his claws. Now he knew something bizarre was going on!

All of a sudden they heard children's screams and the sounds of running feet.

The mothers and fathers started running toward the sounds yelling out their children's names. As they rounded the passageway, they caught sight of children running, yelling and, unbelievable as it seemed, laughing. As they ran up one of the children yelled "Mommy! Daddy! You finally joined the party"!!!

The adults stopped dead in their tracks. "Mary, what in the world are you talking about?" her father practically yelled as he reached out and grabbed her.

All the adults came running up and encircled their children. Mary looked around at all the frantic faces and in a small, scared voice cried, "Well our new friend *Dana invited us to a party. She said not to worry. She said that all the parents knew about the party, and she had invited them as well!"

Mary's mom asked "Where is this Dana now? I want to talk to her!!!"

"Mom she is right there!" Mary said pointing. "Wow! Well, she was right there a second ago. We have been playing hide and seek and a bunch of other fun games with her."

All the parents grabbed and hugged their children with tears of relief. However, there was no Dana to be found.

Lazarus and the others started talking. Many swore that they had heard a little girl's' voice saying *"Come and join the party!"* They all had shrugged it off as their fear fueled imaginations.

Some of the crew started whispering among themselves. Lazarus spotted them and asked what it was that they were saying.

"Well Mr. Lézard sir, there have been many stories, over the years, of the ghost of a young girl passenger. Crew members have seen what they thought was a young girl running and playing in the lower crew areas."

"Many years ago a male passenger had gone mad and killed his wife and children. He then killed himself. One of his daughters was named Dana!"

This story stopped everyone cold. Chills ran up and down many backs as they all looked around with wonder and fear on their faces.

Even with the joy of finding their children safe and no worse for wear, there was still a bizarre feeling of what they had all experienced together. For the remainder of the cruise, the name Dana cropped up around the dinner tables and on into the evenings with snifters of brandy and cigar smoke accenting the air.

Even though the more adventurous souls had fun searching for more ghosts, there were no more to be seen on this trip.

New York Harbor:

Lazarus was looking forward to his upcoming visit with his grandkids Lenny and Lizzie. He hadn't seen them in some years. Now that he was slowing down his duties, as an ambassador to the Far North, he knew it was time to get to know them better.

His wife of so many wonderful years, Lorraine, had passed away five years ago, and he needed his family.

As the days rolled by aboard ship his excitement grew. He loved his home and work, but it kept him far away from his family and especially those two grandkids.

He was finally close enough to feel New York seeping into his bones. Standing at the ship's rail, he could just see the Statue of Liberty. It was materializing through the morning fog which was enveloping the Eastern Seaboard.

This sight never failed to generate excitement in the pit of his stomach. He had spent his youngest years in New York, and the memories rushed back at him in wave upon wave.

These were sweet and sour memories of all those early hardscrabble years. He recalled all the fighting he endured as part of the small lizard minority population that had come to this new country with all their hopes and dreams. Breaking new ground in a new country was difficult. The language barrier was just a small part of it. There had always been a deep-seated mistrust between the Humans and the Lizards.

The ship made its own type of waves as it steamed toward its destination. The piers and terminals were just becoming visible in the distance.

Seagulls, pelicans, and other scavenger birds were circling in huge numbers hoping for a free meal. They raised quite a racket with their squawking and pecking beaks slashing and fighting for their place at the table.

As the ship began its final approach to the dock, Lazarus could feel New York's energy radiating out toward them.

The sound of the tug boats and the smell of diesel only added to the excitement. New York was all consuming in its groundswell of a life lived at the speed of *neon light!

Lazarus was reminded of the downside of this onslaught. He had fought back against prejudice to earn a position of respect among his peers.

Fighting had caused him to leave this country and strike out for the frozen lands of the north. Those travels held dreams of adventure and possible acceptance that he hadn't felt here in his younger years. Such were the dreams of a young lizard.

Having his claws back on American soil felt good. The homesickness he had for his far away home in the North melted away. One more day of train travel would reunite him with his family who now lived further west of New York.

Schoolyard Traumas:

The next day several states away Lenny and Lizzie Lézard were on their school bus heading home. As had happened many times in the past Lenny was protectively holding his sister's hand as she sobbed huge crocodile tears.

The human kids had been at them again with their mean and nasty comments. If Lenny heard *"Lizard Lips"* or *"Reptile Breath"* one more time he knew he would blow his cool. Being a cold-blooded species did not help in this at all.

"Lizzie", Lenny said, "Grandpa Laz should be there when we get home. Don't let those mean kids ruin this day! He will be able to help us. I know he will!"

They had been waiting for this day for so long. They knew that he lived in a far off land that was surrounded by mystery. They had been told so little about his life away from them that they were bubbling over with a million questions.

"He has seen the world. He knows everything!" Lenny said.

"Maybe you're right Lenny. It just hurts when those girls treat me like I'm a snake. **We are not snakes!!!** Can't they see the difference? We have legs and arms just like they do. So what if we have claws! I swear that if that Ashley Ashford cow tries to trip me one more time in the cafeteria, I am going to show here just how interesting having claws can be!!!"

"Now come on Lizzie calling her a cow is just stooping to her level. Call her a pig instead. Have you seen how she gobbles her food? And how about that snorting noise she makes when she laughs?"

This visual picture brought a smile to Lizzie's face, at least for a second.

As they walked up to the door, they had their claws crossed. Maybe Grandpa Laz was already there waiting for them. Lizzie's eyes were still red and swollen from her crying spell, but she tried to put on a happy face.

The door opened, and there he was! "Grandpa, Grandpa" they both cried out as they jumped for joy.

This welcoming was one of those special times in life. Lazarus could see that Lizzie had been crying, but he would wait until later to ask about it. He was just so happy to see them. Seeing their excitement and happiness toward him made him feel many years younger in an instant.

They both jumped into his arms, and he held them as if they were light as feathers. Now he had his crocodile tears running down his snout as well. It seemed like just yesterday that they had hatched from their eggs, and now here they were, just so big.

It made him feel that he had missed a lot of important moments in their lives. Well, he was here to stay for a while. They had so much caught up to do.

It was the start of the weekend. The kids didn't have school for the next two days. They spent all Saturday talking and getting to know each other all over again.

Sunday after church Lazarus took Lenny and Lizzie to the park for a picnic. As they watched the human children running and playing Laz noticed Lizzie seemed a little sad. It reminded him of how she had been crying on Friday when she came in the door from school.

"Lizzie," he asked, "I couldn't help but notice that you were troubled when you came home from school the other day. You seem a little set off by the human kids today. You know I have many years of dealing with this type of stuff. Is there something you want to talk to me about?"

At first, Lizzie tried to brush it aside, but then she broke down and cried into his chest. "Oh, Grandpa I have tried so hard to fit in and be friends with everyone. It's just that some of the human kids act like they hate us for no reason. I don't do anything to cause them to act this way toward me. I am getting to the point where I want to strike back, but that goes against everything my parents have taught me. I don't know what to do!"

As he held her, he thought back to his troubled youth fighting his personal demons dealing with hate and mistrust between the Humans and Lizards.

Lazarus looked at his grandkids and realized again that they were growing up. "Lenny and Lizzy I have some important things I would like to tell the two of you over the next few days. Let's head home and get comfortable by fire. I have a long story to tell"!

Back in their cozy living room Lazarus sat back in a large easy chair and lit his favorite pipe.

"You know Lizzie I think you and Lenny are finally old enough to learn some hidden truths that many Humans and Lizards alike have swept under the carpet of time since the dark days of the far distant past."

Lizzie leaned back giving her Grandfather a searching look. So much of his past was shrouded in mystery. At times, he could say the oddest things. What did he mean? What dark days? What distant past?

Lenny, on the other hand, was buzzing with excitement. He just knew they were in for the story of a lifetime................

*Chapter 1 Endnotes:

- Yukon: The Yukon, a territory in northwest Canada, is wild, mountainous and sparsely populated. It's known for dog-sledding, canoe expeditions, hiking, salmon fishing and other outdoor pursuits, as well as for the colorful northern lights sometimes seen in its nighttime sky. Kluane National Park and Reserve includes Mt. Logan, Canada's highest peak, as well as glaciers, trails, and the Alsek River, renowned for water rafting.

- RMS Queen Mary is a retired ocean liner that sailed primarily on the North Atlantic Ocean from 1936 to 1967 for the Cunard Line (known as Cunard-White Star Line when the vessel entered service). Built by John Brown and Company in Clydebank, Scotland, Queen Mary along with her running mate, the RMS Queen Elizabeth, were built as part of Cunard's planned two-ship weekly express service between Southampton, Cherbourg, and New York City. The two ships were a British response to the superliners built by German and French companies in the late 1920s and early 1930s. Queen Mary was the flagship of the Cunard Line from May 1936 until October 1946 when she was replaced in that role by Queen Elizabeth.
Queen Mary sailed on her maiden voyage on 27 May 1936 and captured the Blue Riband in August of that year; she lost the title to SS Normandie in 1937 and recaptured it in 1938, holding it until 1952 when she was beaten by the new SS United States. With the outbreak of World War II, she was converted into a troopship and ferried Allied soldiers for the duration of the war.
Following the war, Queen Mary was refitted for passenger service and along with Queen Elizabeth commenced the

two-ship transatlantic passenger service for which the two ships were initially built. The two ships dominated the transatlantic passenger transportation market until the dawn of the jet age in the late 1950s. By the mid-1960s, Queen Mary was aging and, though still among the most popular transatlantic liners, was operating at a loss.

- **Queen Mary**: Now a Haunted Floating Hotel: Internationally recognized, the historic floating hotel and museum attracts thousands of visitors every year. It has also attracted some unearthly guests over the years. In fact, some say the Queen Mary is one of the most haunted places in the world with as many as 150 known spirits lurking upon the ship. Over the past 60 years, the Queen Mary has been the site of at least 49 reported deaths, not to mention having gone through the terrors of war, so it comes as no surprise that spectral spirits of her vivid past continue to walk within her rooms and hallways.

Located 50 feet below water level is the Queen Mary's engine room, which is said to be a hotbed of paranormal activity. Used in the filming of the Poseidon Adventure, the room's infamous "Door 13" crushed at least two men to death, at different points during the ship's history. The most recent death, during a routine watertight door drill in 1966, crushed an 18-year-old crew member. The young man was dressed in blue coveralls and sported a beard. He has often been spied walking the length of Shaft Alley before disappearing by door #13.

- The Ghost Dana: A young girl who was murdered possibly in B-474 with her entire family by her father. Her two little sisters and mother were found strangled on the bed while Dana and her father were found dying in their bathroom with gunshot wounds. Dana now likes to play in the cargo area and is also heard calling for her mother. Dana has often been heard in the boiler room and even in the second class pool area.

- Kasbah Arabic, or in older English Casbah, and qassabah or qassabah in India, is a type of medina, Islamic city, or fortress (citadel).
It was a place for the local leader to live and defense when a city was under attack. A Kasbah has high walls, usually without windows. Sometimes, they were built on hilltops so that they could be easily defended. They placed some near the entrance to harbors.

- **Brief History of Neon:** Over the last 150 years the luminous tube industry has evolved from the simple laboratory experiments in the second half of the 19th century to an industry of worldwide proportions. The first luminous tubes did not use neon or any other rare gas. In the late 1800's scientist developed reliable and somewhat safe high voltage supplies and began running high voltages through many things to observe what would happen. Often, they tested to see how wide of an air gap the spark could jump. It was quickly observed that the spark gap was inversely proportional to the pressure of the air, and it soon became apparent, that an evacuated glass tube was the ideal method for viewing light from gas discharges.
When British researcher William Ramsey discovered the five rare gasses between 1894-98, receiving the Noble Prize in 1904, it became possible for a French scientist, Georges Claude, to note that noble gasses could be made to produce light discharges when electrical discharges were passed through them. It was the method that scientists had been looking for, a form of practical lighting by glowworm or

phosphorescent light, "Light without Heat."

By World War l, Claude had acquired many patents, but he had more on his mind than strictly scientific knowledge. He envisioned a lucrative market for his tubes in lighting and signage. Because neon gas produced the brightest light, it was used almost exclusively, and soon the generic "Neon Sign", was born. By 1924, "Claude Neon" franchises appeared in 14 major cities across the United States. And in 1927, out of a total of 750 neon signs in New York City, 611 had been made by Claude Neon Lights, Inc.

There was a great period of creativity for neon in the years that followed, a period when many design and animation techniques developed. Unfortunately, the economic conditions caused by the depression slowed neon's growth. However, one place neon did work its magic during this period, was on the exteriors of movie palaces, providing a colorfully glowing invitation to the fantasy world within. Following World War ll, and the advent of plastics, manufacturers began promoting Plexiglas shadow boxes with fluorescent lighting, neon's cousin, bchind lettering and graphics. Neon was considered old fashioned. This then relegated it to being used as a hidden light source. Today still, 75% of neon is used in this way.

During the last decade, neon has seen a rebirth, and artist, architects, and interior designers are beginning to rediscover its exciting possibilities. One day, city planners will recognize neon's value as an element of urban vitality, and come to realize that the bleakness of city centers is due, in part, to the absence of this colorful element. Neon tube construction hasn't changed much since the days of Claude Neon. It's still a handcrafted medium, and a glass bender heats and forms each letter one bend at a time. However, the state of the art components and much-improved equipment make the neon tube of today, superior to its predecessor.

Chapter 2
Mail or Jail

As they all relaxed back with the sweet smell of pipe smoke hazing the air. Grandpa Laz took a few minutes to collect his thoughts. Giving the kids the story of his life was incredibly important to get right. His far-away look piqued their curiosity. Lenny, impatient as always, was about to blurt out something, but Lizzie placed a restraining hand on his shoulder. With a claw to her lips, she beseeched him to wait a moment.

They noticed grandpa's demeanor take on a much younger cast as he dug way back into his youth.

Finally, with a deep sigh he began:

"When I was not much more than a hatchling, much younger than the two of you are now, my parents, your great grandparents, were forced to move part of the family from our ancestral home in Europe to New York in the hopes of more work to put food on the table. Times were tough, and they could not bring everyone all at the same time." Grandpa Laz became a little sad with the recollection.

He continued; "Those early days in Europe were extremely bad for Lizards and Humans alike. My parents could not afford to bring the whole family at the same time. Some of my siblings, like my brother Lorenzo, had to remain behind with our relatives in France. This separation ripped the family apart."

An extremely sad look came over Lazarus as he remembered how hard this choice had been for his parents. It was several years before the family could reunite. His earliest memories of his mother were watching her hide the tears that were always so close to the surface. She tried so hard not to show this, but it was always there.

"At least, the father could find work at the New York docks and shipyards. Life was hard, but we moved on. Finally, my parents saved enough to bring my brother and two sisters to our new home."

"We were in school by then. It was very hard on your uncle, Lorenzo. He missed his cousins and friends that he had gone to school with in Paris. Lizards were treated more like equals there in those days. This situation just made it harder for him to fit into this new life."

He always talked about moving back there someday to go to college in Europe. "As you kids know he gained fame as a newspaper journalist during the World Wars I and II. There are many exciting stories about Lorenzo during those days, but those are stories for another time. Needless to say, the whole family is very proud of him."

"Back in the early days, it was much harder on us to try to fit in. I know you will find this hard to believe Lizzie, but it was much worse than it is today. The humans did not like all the Lizards coming to what they considered as their personal city and taking jobs away from them."

"This made for bad blood, whether warm or cold blooded. The human kids heard their parents grumbling about this and it made it easy for them to take it out of us in the schoolyard. We were different, and that was a good enough reason for them to gang up on us."

"I learned later in life that the mistrust between humans and lizards had a much deeper history. That history always seemed to bubble just under all our conscious thoughts. Deeply buried sparks of a war between early man and a large flying reptile was included in a few writings from ancient manuscripts. These ideas were scratched off as stories told late at night to scare the kids."

"Also, keep in mind that human kids outnumbered us one hundred to one in those early days. This situation always kept us on edge. It made me feel very alone."

"Once Lorenzo finally came home to us I had someone to watch my back. We were forced to learn many types of self-defense techniques. We spent all our time practicing boxing and King Fu. The humans had numbers on their side, but we were not defenseless. Our claws and especially our tails could do a lot of damage."

Lenny jumped up and shouted, *"You go, Grandpa!"*

Laz sat him back down, "Now hold on a minute Lenny. There is so much more to this history lesson than an "**Eye for an Eye**". History will prove to you that there are much better ways to deal with problems then causing harm to someone else."

"Somehow we made it through high school alive and not in jail for killing someone."

"Lorenzo had had enough of New York. After many hours of talking and head scratching he decided that it was time to return to Europe University. We still had many relatives there, and he had stayed in touch with his friends from his earlier days. He spoke some foreign languages, so it was kind of like a homecoming for him."

"It was a sad day for me when I had to say goodbye to Lorenzo for the second time in my life. I was desperately lonely. I no longer had my backup, and it felt like everyone was my enemy."

"I did get in a couple of years of college. I thought I might follow Lorenzo eventually to Europe, so I studied some languages. They came quickly to me because my parents also spoke several languages. Of course, they pushed us to become fluent in English, but French and German did feel second nature to me."

"I was still getting into more and more trouble due to fighting back against any slight that came my way. As time went on, the fights became far more dangerous to both me and my opponents. The human kids were now human adults and the hatred was becoming lethal between the races. These conflicts were at the beginning of the 1890's and with more lizards coming here to find work and a new start the fighting escalated. The court system and constables came to know me by my street name of Lasher Lézard!"

Lenny wanted to yell out *"Lasher Lézard"* but Lazarus held up a hand to stop him again.

"After one particularly bloody confrontation, I was thrown in jail!"

"Oh, Grandpa" exclaimed Lizzie, "How awful. What happened?"

"Well honey, I hurt someone, so I was locked up and then hauled in front of a judge. He could have sent me off to prison for a long time, but he had an interesting option for me. This judge had relatives trying to build an infrastructure for the burgeoning population rushing to the new gold strikes in the Yukon Territories of Northwest Canada and into Alaska." Grandpa Laz talked about history in a way that Lenny and Lizzie found fascinating.

The judge said "They need everything up there! Everything from store clerks to cooks, from carpenters to cowboys, from painters to plumbers."

"It is a melting pot. Think about it; all languages and species are working together and building a new International community. With your background in languages and your obvious ability to fight your way through and around things, you would be perfect as a mail carrier."

"A mail carrier?" Lazarus cried out. "You want me to go to the frigid Far North to deliver mail to a bunch of crazy miners? *In the Snow?"* He felt a chill travel over his tail and up his back. The term Melting Pot shouldn't be in the same sentence. All he could picture was ice and snow. "You're trying to turn me into a greensicle." he sputtered.

"Well, Lazarus" the judge replied. "There is always a nice warm, dry jail cell here you can have!!!" "Besides," he continued, "This is much more than just delivering mail. You would be the backbone of communications in a whole new land. It seems that you need some practice in communicating with more than just your fists and that lethal tail of yours! The next time you could be in front of me for murder! I don't see that you have much of a choice here. If you sign a contract to spend three years there, I will take this offense out of your permanent record!"

"So which is it son, your tail in jail? Or a paid vacation of adventure and excitement near the North Pole? Who knows you may end up thinking of me as Santa Claus for this gift I am offering you!"

Lazarus said; "Can I think about this?" The judge said "No! You have wasted enough of this court's time over the past few years. Take it now or it is off to jail with you!"

Lenny and Lizzie were mesmerized. Their imaginations soared as their Grandpa's story continued to unfold.

Chapter 3
Long Trips and Long Johns

The court gave Lazarus a month to get his affairs in order. An agent contacted Laz, from Seattle, Washington by a Mr. Allen Derby, who was the West Coast representative of his future boss Jean-Paul "Frenchie" LeBlanc. Frenchie was the head man for a private company doing business in *Dawson, a town in the Yukon Territory.

Mr. Derby made arrangements to send tickets, travel directions, and general information to Lazarus. Mr. Derby wrote that he would meet with Laz upon his arrival in Seattle.

Laz was told that it would be an arduous trip, but once in Dawson, he would be outfitted with everything he would need to live in the hostile environment of the Far North.

To prepare for the trip, he was told to pack for cold weather and not to forget the Long Johns. That was not as easy as it sounds. Lizard long johns could not be located on every street corner, but his mother was quite a seamstress.

On the other hand finding things like lizard friendly gloves and snow boots wasn't as big a problem. There were more and more stores that catered to the growing lizard population. He had been given clothing and travel allotment. They had thought of everything which made him feel better about what lay ahead.

He started spending most of his time at the university library. He figured that if he was to make it through this coming ordeal, he needed to know as much as possible about survival in harsh climates.

He studied everything from building igloos to dog sledding. Did bears like the taste of lizard? He could not find any information on that. Hopefully, green meat wouldn't appeal to them.

He went to a gun range and practiced with pistols, rifles, especially big bore rifles. He had no intention of ending up as bear breakfast, bear lunch or any grizzly snack.

The more he learned about this new land, the safer and more secure that jail cell started looking. What scared him the most was the lack of information to study about that part of the world. It reminded him of the old saying; "What you don't know could kill you"! He wasn't keen on this trailblazing stuff.

Trailblazing with Lorenzo in Paris sounded like a lot more fun than the ordeal that was in store for him.

Just getting there could take months depending on the weather. The travel time changed his three-year contract into more like three and a half when you factored in the travel time each way.

Hugs and Hard Goodbyes:

Long trips usually have something in common. They start with sad goodbyes.

It was finally time to leave. The family, who were still in New York, all boarded a horse-drawn Trolley and headed to Grand Central Terminal to shed tears and wave Lazarus off on the first leg of his long journey.

Not knowing if he would ever see his family again was almost more than any of them could stand. They were a strong lot and did have a history of sad farewells, but it was still extremely difficult.

As the train wheels began to roll along the miles Lazarus' mood rolled over as well. The sadness disappeared and was replaced by an electrical charge of excitement. He was now headed toward the great unknown. He could barely get his mind around what lay ahead for him. It was beyond anything he could even begin to imagine.

He wondered if his father had experienced these same mixed emotions as the family steamed out of Europe on that ship so many years ago.

Leaving loved ones behind was hard, but he was also so completely overwhelmed by thoughts of what lay ahead that it left no room for sadness.

Laz began weighing out his abilities.He counted off the pros and cons of what he could do. He knew he needed to stay positive for what lay ahead.

He had studied as much as he could dig up on the *Klondike, the Yukon and the town of Dawson. He knew there was some French, Russian and Asian languages spoken in the Far North Country. With a Gold Rush, raging people were coming there from all points of the world's compass. He knew some languages and was a quick learner when it came to them. He had even read up on what he could find on the Inuit Indians spoken tongue.

With his background in martial arts and his firearms practice, he felt physically ready for anything that could be thrown at him as well. Well, maybe not the bears! For some reason, he had visions of forests full of lizard chomping fanged behemoths with the "Lazarus Lunch Special" at the top of their menus.

Lazarus had plenty of time to ponder what was on his menu. It ended taking about 40 hours on the *New York Central RR to get to Chicago. It seemed that the train stopped at every little community hub along the rail line. Very few lizards traveled by rail in those days so he got plenty of curious looks. Some were hostile, but he was used to that. Most humans just looked away quickly when he turned in their direction.

What he did notice was that the further west he traveled the most open his fellow passengers seemed to be. More and more included him in conversations.

He started feeling more comfortable in the presence of these humans. This was a whole new experience for Lazarus. There were fewer and fewer business types with more farmers, teachers, and construction workers coming aboard.

Everyone that heard where Laz was headed had tons of questions. It made for exciting and stimulating conversation. Everyone was interested in what was happening in the gold fields. They all seemed to know someone who had gone or wanted to go and try their luck at the fortune just lying around in riverbeds to be scooped up.

In Chicago, he transferred to the *Burlington and Missouri RR headed to Council Bluffs, Iowa. Every curve in the track brought new vistas of lands he had not seen before except in scratchy Tintype photos and paintings.

Crossing the Union Pacific Bridge over the Missouri River was quite a thrill. Seeing the huge expanse of water far below was breathtaking. Everywhere he turned there were new thrills and experiences to be soaked up.

The train stopped in Omaha, Nebraska where the passengers, that were heading further West disembarked to spend the night at the historical *Millard Hotel.

He didn't want just to sit in his room alone. The excitement of his travels and the thoughts of where he was going was enough to keep him energized and a little too hyper to sleep.

With Lazarus' gift for languages, he decided to wander over to the Little Italy section of downtown Omaha. Another traveler that he had met had told him about it.

His name was *Sebastiano Salerno. He and his brother *Joseph were also immigrants just like Laz's family.

Although he was human, the two of them had much in common. They struck up a great rolling conversation about Europe and what immigrants had to deal with in their new country.

Sebastiano and his family were pivotal in establishing Little Italy in the Omaha area.

He was fascinated by the direction Laz's travels were taking him. He invited Laz to meet with him and his brother that night at an Italian restaurant.

Laz decided to take him up on the invitation and without realizing it, he began to build a worldwide network of friends and associates that would be of real importance to him later in his life.

The Salerno Brothers lived near the Union Pacific railroad yards in downtown Omaha. Sebastiano worked as an agent for a steamship company. The company did business all over the world and once goods arrived they needed to be shipped by land. The two brothers knew a lot about worldwide transportation and communications. Between the three of them, they had contacts, friends, and family all over Europe and the United States

They talked into the late night hours and traded contact information. They agreed to stay in touch over the following years. The brothers were interested in Lazarus' future travels in the Far North and made him promise to send them letters whenever he could.

Westward Bound:

Early the next morning Lazarus boarded a Union Pacific RR car heading west. They started passing through more wide open spaces. This country would prove to be on the Wild West side of things judging by the look of some of his fellow passengers.

Some were obviously cowboys. They had trouble walking down the narrow aisles between the seats due to their bowed legs and their huge 10-gallon hats. You could tell that they spent more time on horseback than on trains. He had heard all the noise and commotion their horses had raised as they were led onto special boxcars.

The more he was around these men, the more curious he became. He had read that Cowboys were an especially taciturn breed, but these men seemed particularly observant and tough.

He struck up a conversation with one of them who was a little more outgoing than the rest. It turned out that they had martial arts in common, and they discussed techniques for hours on end. On several rest stops, the train made along the way; they practiced interesting karate moves.

Lazarus' new friend *Charles "Charlie" Siringo was especially interested in learning defensive moves to counter the tail sweeps Laz snuck in on him.

Over the next few days of train travel, they cemented a friendship that would last for years. Charlie was about 20 years older, and Laz looked to him over the coming years as a mentor. Of course, at this time, Laz thought that Charlie was just a really interesting cowboy.

The Lincoln County War:

He had stories about other friends like *Sheriff Pat Garrett, who had become famous for his shootout with *Billy, the Kid. These events all happened during the *Lincoln County War. It was a giant range war over cattle ranching. (See Chapter 3 Endnotes)

Laz did notice that Charlie always remained vigilant and on edge. He always kept his eyes moving and seemed to watch the other passengers with a penetrating look in his eye.

During the second day of the trip, there was a loud commotion in one of the forward train cars. Laz heard gun shots. He also saw all the Cowboys running towards the rear of the train where their trained handlers were saddling their horses.

Out of the Pullman car windows, Laz could see riders moving in on the train from across the prairie. He watched a fellow passenger pull a gun and aim it toward Charlie's back. Without thinking Laz used his tail in a lightning quick Kung Fu type move which knocked the pistol out of the back shooter's hand and across the floor.

His friend Charlie pulled out a badge and yelled to Laz, "Hold him," he yelled. "He is a train robber, and we are here to stop them!"

Down the track, there was movement from a box car. Laz's snout dropped open at an amazing sight. Horses and riders were flying out through a specially equipped boxcar's open sliding door and heading out to match firepower with the bandits. Dust was flying, and gunfire filled the air as the cowardly bandits took to their heels.

The passengers were all cheering as Laz held the sniveling crook by the back of his shirt and the seat of his pants.

"Quit wiggling or I'll snap your ugly head right off of your skinny chicken neck. You were going to shoot my friend right in the back without a chance! I wouldn't want to be you when he gets back from rounding up your pathetic partners in crime!"

"Tell me now!!! Where there any more of you back-shooting cowards on board pretending to be passengers?"

The train robber tried to clam up, but a few well-placed claws to his backside were wonderful tools to loosen lips.

After a few serious claw marks to the seat of his pants, the crook started spilling the beans. "There were two others," he blubbered, "One to stop the train and another to do the same thing I was supposed to do."

"You mean to shoot someone else in the back?" Lazarus exclaimed shaking him like a noodle!!! The crook answered by wetting his pants right in front of everybody.

"EEwwwww," a young girl cried out as a yellow puddle began to spread across the floor of the train car.

With the help of some of the other passengers Laz hogtied their prisoner to a seat. They then swept the other train cars searching for the two other undercover crooks.

They were thrilled to find that they were not the only passengers that didn't just lie down to the bad men.

In the third car up from theirs, they found another group of passengers beating a crook up and down the aisles. They almost hated to stop them, but this outlaw was headed for far worse once the lawmen got their hands on him.

When they got to the train engine, they found the engineer in full control of the train. The bumbling crook who was supposed to take over driving the train had tripped over a coal shovel and stumbled down the steps breaking his arm, leg and three ribs. Well so much for the best-laid plans of Mice and Men!!! As always; "Crime Does Not Pay!!!"

By the time they had bandaged up the low down and dirty robber, he had looked like a mummy! He was crying out for help. The first aid work might have been just a tad overzealous.

Lazarus asked; "Oh is that bandage a little too tight for you Mr. Train Robber?? Here let me give it another yank!" Screams for help bounced off the walls of the engine compartment. "There now isn't that much better?" Lazarus said as he smiled with sympathy.

Cowboys with Badges:

After a few hours, the officers returned with what remained of the ragtag bunch of criminals. Lazarus turned over the bandaged and hogtied crooks to his new friend Charlie.

They wrapped up the now ex-train robbers and locked them in a jail cell that that was in the special boxcar. This operation was in the works for several years. It was designed to bag what remained of the gangs that had been robbing trains and banks ever since the end of the Civil War.

Charlie, it turned out, was the lead officer. Over the years, he had been a well-respected cowboy in Texas, a Lawman and a Pinkerton Agency Detective. He made a name for himself chasing rustlers and train robbers all over the west.

Many years later Charlie and Lazarus worked together again, in Idaho. They moderated troubles between the mine owners and the United Mine Workers Union, who were at each other's throats.

This adventure was Lazarus' first foray into being on the right side of the law, and he liked it. Feeling the appreciation of the other passengers toward him was extremely rewarding.

Laz had always been taught to do the right thing, but years of the prejudice he had grown up with had pushed him to fight back. Saving humans was a whole new side of life for him.

*Chapter 3 Endnotes:

- The Klondike: This is a region of the Yukon Territories in northwest Canada, east of the Alaskan border. It lies near the Klondike River, a small river that enters the Yukon River from the east at Dawson City.

  The Klondike is famed because of the Klondike Gold Rush, which started in 1897 and lasted until 1899. Gold has been mined continuously in that area except for a hiatus in the late 1960s and early 1970s.

  The name "Klondike" evolved from the Hän word *Tr'ondëk*, which means "hammerstone water." Early gold seekers found it difficult to pronounce the First Nations word, so "Klondike" was the result of this poor pronunciation.

- New York Central RR: The New York Central Railroad, known simply as the New York Central in its publicity, was a railroad operating in the Northeastern United States. It began construction in approximately 1826. Headquartered in New York City, the railroad served most of the Northeast, including extensive trackage in the states of New York, Pennsylvania, Ohio, Michigan, Indiana, Illinois, and Massachusetts, plus additional trackage in the Canadian provinces of Ontario and Quebec.

  The railroad primarily connected greater New York and Boston in the east with Chicago and St. Louis in the Midwest along with the intermediate cities of Albany, Buffalo, Cleveland, Cincinnati, and Detroit. NYC's Grand Central Terminal in New York City is one of its best-known extant landmarks.

Burlington and Missouri RR: The Burlington and Missouri River Railroad came together in Burlington, Iowa in 1852. It commenced operations on January 1, 1856, with only a few miles of track. In 1857 it connected to Ottumwa, followed by Murray in 1858. It finally reached the Missouri River in November 1859. It used wood-burning locomotives and wooden passenger cars.

- Millard Hotel: Following the Grand Central Hotel disaster, Omaha was once again without a top-flight hotel. The Millard Hotel opened to the public in July of 1882, was designed to fill this void. It was a five-story building located on the northeast corner of 13th and Douglas Streets. The Millard was one of the representative establishments and a prominent feature of Omaha. Being a first-class hotel it has no superior in the West, combining in a perfect manner comfort, elegance, and convenience" (*Pen and Sunlight Sketches*, p. 83). In its earliest days of existence, the Millard "waged a duel for supremacy" with the Paxton Hotel (which was built on the site of the former Grand Central Hotel) ["7 Dead in Hotel Fire", p. 2]. It was claimed that "absolutely no danger from fire" (*Omaha Illustrated*, p. 60) existed at the Millard. Unfortunately, this did not prove to be accurate. On February 8, 1933 – when temperatures reached fifteen degrees below zero – a disastrous fire started at the Millard Hotel. By the time the blaze was contained, seven firefighters had died, and twenty-two more were injured.

- Joseph and Sebastiano Salerno: Omaha's first Italian enclave developed during the 1890s near the intersection of South 24th Street and Poppleton Street. It was formed by immigrants from southern Italy and migrants from eastern American cities. Two brothers, Joseph and Sebastiano Salerno, are credited with creating Little Italy, located further north near the Union Pacific yards in downtown. When Sebastiano took a job as an agent for a steamship company in 1904, he encouraged friends from Sicily to emigrate. Joseph then secured boarding and jobs for the immigrants, particularly in downtown Omaha's Union Pacific shops. In 1905, Sicilian immigrants settled along South 6th Street in the hills south of downtown. Additional waves of Sicilians arrived between 1912 and 1913 and following World War I.[5] South 10th Street was also particularly important to the Italian community.

- **Charles "Charlie" Siringo:**
  He was a Cowboy, Lawman, Pinkerton

Agent, and one of the first undercover Lawmen in the west. Charlie even worked for a time as a merchant.
In 1886, bored with the mundane life of a merchant, Siringo moved to Chicago. His first-hand observation of the city's labor conflict (which he attributed to foreign anarchism) moved him to

join the Pinkerton Detective Agency, using gunman *Pat Garrett's name as a reference to get the job; having met Garrett several years before. With 2,000 active agents and 30,000 reserves, the forces of the Pinkerton National Detective Agency were larger than the nation's standing army in the late-19th century. The Pinkertons provided services for management in labor disputes, including armed guards and secret operatives like Charles A. Siringo.

He was immediately assigned several cases, which took him as far north as Alaska, and as far south as Mexico City. He began operating undercover, a relatively new technique at the time, and infiltrated gangs of robbers and rustlers, making over one hundred arrests.

- Patrick Floyd Jarvis "Pat" Garrett was an  American Old West lawman, bartender and customs agent who became renowned for killing Billy the Kid. He was also the sheriff of Lincoln County, New Mexico as well as Doña Ana County, New Mexico. At 6' 5" he was another larger than life figure of the Old West, who also died by gunshot. He left behind eight children.

- Billy the Kid was made famous as an American Old West gunfighter. He participated in New Mexico's Lincoln County

War and is known to have killed eight men. Sheriff Pat Garrett killed him.

- The **Lincoln County War** was an Old West conflict between rival factions in 1878 in New Mexico Territory. The feud became famous because of the participation of some notable figures of the Old West, including Billy the Kid, sheriffs William Brady and Pat Garrett, cattle rancher John Chisum, lawyer and businessman Alexander McSween, and the organized-crime boss Lawrence Murphy.
The conflict arose between two factions over the control of dry goods and cattle interests in the county. The older, established faction was led by Murphy and his business partner, James Dolan, who operated a dry goods monopoly through Murphy's general store. Young newcomers to the county, English-born John Tunstall, and his business partner Alexander McSween, with backing from established cattleman John Chisum, opened a competing store in 1876. The two sides gathered lawmen, businessmen, Tunstall's ranch hands and criminal gangs to their support. The Murphy-Dolan faction was allied with Lincoln County Sheriff Brady, and supported by the Jesse Evans Gang. The Tunstall-McSween faction organized their posse of armed men, known as the Regulators, to defend their position, and had their lawmen, town constable Richard M. Brewer and Deputy US Marshal Robert A.

Widenmann.

The conflict was marked by back-and-forth revenge killings, starting with the murder of Tunstall by members of the Evans Gang. In revenge for this, the Regulators killed Sheriff Brady and others in a series of incidents. Further killings continued unabated for several months, climaxing in the Battle of Lincoln, a five-day gunfight, and siege that resulted in the death of McSween and the scattering of the Regulators. After Pat Garrett had been named County Sheriff in 1880, he hunted down Billy the Kid, killing two other former Regulators in the process. The war has been fictionalized in several Hollywood films, including Sam Peckinpah's Pat Garrett and Billy the Kid, The Left Handed Gun in 1958, John Wayne's Chisum in 1970 and Young Guns in 1988.

Chapter 4
Indian Territory
Cheyenne, Wyoming:

The next morning the train pulled into what started to feel like the real Wild West of his imagination. Looking out the train car windows Laz could make out a rainbow spectrum of individuals and garb walking by. There were, of course, cowboys, and then he saw some Chinese with their pointed bamboo hats. He saw a few African Americans and Mexican men and women in their distinctive serapes and dresses. These people came from all walks of life.

He was pleasantly surprised to see a family of Lizards that looked like they dressed for a nice day out on the town.

What stood him up on his claws for a closer look was his first view of real live American Indians walking down the street. They had feathers and beads in their hair. This sight was mind blowing stuff!!! Of course, he had seen pictures of them and had read tons of books about them in the past, but this was the first ones he had ever seen in the flesh, feathers and all! Wow!!!

Most of the others like the African Americans and Chinese he had seen in New York and Paris. But never any real live Indians.

He was always fascinated by skin color, his being green after all. They actually did have a well-tanned slightly red highlight to their skin. This was amazing to him, and he really hoped he might meet one or two.

He did have a two-day layover in Cheyenne. This layover could prove to be a very interesting interlude.

He mentioned all this to Charlie, and he said he would be glad to introduce him around. Charlie had spent a lot of time in Cheyenne and knew some of the Plains Indian's that he considered friends.

Charlie and the other officers were busy offloading their prisoners, horses, and gear. They arranged to meet for dinner later.

Lazarus checked into the *Inter-Ocean Hotel. That was an interesting name. Possibly it was named for the areas huge oceans of long grass filled prairies. Seeing the large herds of buffalo flowing across the grassy plains reminded him of schools of porpoise gliding across the ocean waves.

In the lobby, he was surprised to be tracked down by *Ed Towse, a reporter for the Cheyenne Daily Sun.

Ed had run into Charlie at the Sheriff's office. Charlie had told him about Lazarus and said to look him up for a good story.

Ed had made a name for himself as a reporter during the bloody *Johnson County War in the 1880's and early 1890's.

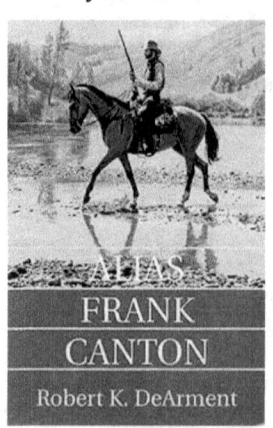 This was a famous range war pitting large cattle ranchers' against their smaller competitors.

The large ranches had power and money. They hired gunslingers who masqueraded in the guise of peacekeepers. Bloodthirsty *Frank M. Canton, the former Sheriff of Johnson County, was hired to lead the band of killers.

This period was a bad time in Montana and Wyoming. Many people were hanged, like rustlers, on dubious evidence. Most notably *Jim Averell, a Johnson County businessman, was lynched in 1889 for cattle rustling, although he owned no cattle.

They didn't stop with just men either. The same day they lynched *Ella "Cattle Kate" Watson. Her only crime was verbally going up against the large ranchers.

Laz had heard about this from reading New York newspapers of the time. It really brought back the understanding that he was in "The Wild West" now! He wondered just how much wilder his final destination was going to be than this.

Ed was fascinated by what he had heard from Charlie Siringo. Over lunch, he asked Laz a thousand questions about what had happened on the train and about his future work in the Far North Country.

As it turned out, due to Ed's work as a newspaper reporter, he could tell Laz more about Dawson and the Gold Rush than Laz knew himself. They had a lively discussion that lasted hours.

Ed gave a letter of introduction to a woman he knew in Dawson. *Belinda Mulrooney had made a big name for herself in the Gold Fields around Dawson. Ed said that she would be a great contact for him.

Miss Mulrooney later became famous for many things including owning mines, hotels and supplying provisions to the other miners. That is where the real money was made in the Gold Rush. She became known as the richest woman in the Klondike.

That evening Laz met with Charlie for dinner. He was surprised to see an elderly distinguished looking Indian

gentleman sitting at the table. Charlie introduced Laz to
***Wovoka** known locally as Jack Wilson.

Over the dinner conversation, Laz
learned that Wovoka was a Paiute Indian
Prophet. He was a peacemaker for his
people.

After experiencing a vision during a
solar eclipse, Wovoka defined a new
religion combining Christian and Native
elements. In the vision, Wovoka was given a glimpse of the
afterlife. If they wished to reach it, God's message was for
the Native peoples to love each other, to not fight, and to live
in peace.

Wovoka was a powerful Medicine Man and the founder
of the *Ghost Dance Movement, which gained widespread
acceptance among Native Americans.

During the next few days, Laz spent a lot of time talking
with Wovoka. These conversations would be of immense
importance to Lazarus' future dealings with the Inuit People
(Eskimos) of the Far North.

He also showed Laz some amazing magic tricks that he
was adept at. With a wink, Wovoka said a few magic tricks
could be of value while spreading God's words for peace.

Wovoka spoke of Indian legends that sounded like
fantasies to Lazarus's young mind. Wovoka wove a spiritual
history of the Far North that dealt with Fire Dragons that
had lived on the earth for many thousands of years.

The way the Indian Spiritualist spoke Lazarus had no
doubt that Wovoka believed in what he was talking about.

Wovoka saw in Lazarus's demeanor that there was a lot
of doubt there. He just smiled and patted Laz on the back.
He said; "There are many wonders in store for you Lazarus.
I envy your pursuit of them in the coming months."

The following morning Laz met with Ed at the Newspaper's office to say goodbye as he was leaving early the following morning.

He mentioned Wovoka's stories and Ed, with a look of interest said; "What a minute, there is an excerpt from something I just read. I want you to read it." He went to his large rack of files and dug around. "OK here it is," handing a newspaper clipping to Laz:

On April 26, 1890, the Tombstone Epitaph (a local Arizona newspaper) reported that two cowboys had discovered and shot down a creature – described as a "winged dragon" – which resembled a pterodactyl, only MUCH larger. The Cowboys said its wingspan was 160 feet, and that its body was more than four feet wide and 92 feet long. The Cowboys supposedly cut off the end of the wing to prove the existence of the creature. The paper's description of the animal fits the *Quetzalcoatlus, whose fossils had been dug up in Texas.

Could this be Thunderbird or Wakinyan, the jagged-winged, fierce-toothed flying creature of Sioux American Indian legend? This Thunderbird supposedly lived in a cave on the top of the Olympic Mountains and feasted on seafood. Different from the Eagle (Wanbli) or Hawk (Cetan) the Wakinyan was said to be huge, carrying off children, and earned its name because of its association with thunder and lightning–supposedly being struck by lightning and seen to fall to the ground during a storm. The monster was further distinguished by its piercing cry and thunderous beating wings.

Note from Author: Above is from an actual Newspaper article of the time! The above Jpeg was not part of that article.

After Laz finished reading Ed continued; "Now I am not saying this did or didn't happen and not just some skullduggery thought up by a couple of whiskey-eyed cowboys, but there are many stories and legends involving dragons and flying reptiles. Your people have stories of where the Lizard population originated from. Just food for thought, but I find it fascinating, to say the least!"

The following morning Laz woke up surprised and a little embarrassed to see his picture and story in the local paper. He had become a minor celebrity and was being called a hero for saving Charlie's life and capturing some of the crooks.

The Townspeople couldn't get enough of the story, and it put the local lizard community in good standing for years to come.

What Laz didn't know was that his story would be picked up by other newspapers around the country, and his family would read about him all the way back in New York.

Of course, the newsmen at the New York Times already knew Lazarus through his brother Lorenzo and their rescue of the Chinese women from the Tong Gangs in Chinatown. (*See Book 2 of The Lézard Family Chronicles.)

His mother could have strangled him for putting himself in such danger, but they were all extremely proud of him.

Laz had met a few Indians from other tribes while he was in Cheyenne. The Plains Indians had a long and distinguished past. They could be ferocious fighters as General *George Custer found out the hard way.

The tribes, who were all part of the Algonquin Indians, were an extremely proud people, and they had been treated very poorly and pushed way too far. Their only recourse was to push back. When they did, it was a sight to behold.

Laz was glad that he was becoming friends with them and not their enemy.

All too soon it was time for Laz to board the train heading further west. It brought tears to his eyes to see how many people showed up to wave goodbye to him. Laz was learning the value of doing good deeds. Making friends with humans was far easier than he could have ever imagined. All it took was a change in perception. A smile versus a snarl cut through prejudice quickly, like a warm knife through butter. In the past, he had thought of only one good use for a knife or a claw. His thoughts were changing, and he liked how it felt.

He and Charlie had become close friends in a very short time. Charlie would never forget that Laz had saved his life by stopping a cowardly back shooter on the train.

Wovoka, along with several other Indians, was among the well-wishers and Laz was also happy to see how many Lizard families had shown up as well. He had a chance to meet some them during his short time in Cheyenne.

Laz had a large number of names and contact info to take with him. He promised to write to them all.

As Grandpa Laz took a break in his storytelling, to open the picnic basket they had brought from the park earlier, Lenny and Lizzie sat back in awe. Where would this exciting story lead to next? They didn't need leftover food. They wanted him to keep spinning this wonderful tale of adventure!!!

*Chapter 4 Endnotes:

- Inter-Ocean Hotel: The Inter-Ocean Hotel, 1436 16th Street, graced the corner of 16th and Blake Streets for one hundred years. Opening to the public on October 29, 1873, the hotel was the creation of Denver pioneer Barney Ford— Colorado's most prominent black businessman. William N. Byers, the editor of the *Rocky Mountain News*, proclaimed it "the finest in the territory and the best-appointed hotel west of Saint Louis."

- Ed Towse: Journalist for the Cheyenne Ledger and the Cheyenne Sun made his name during Wyoming's Johnson County Range Wars.

- The Johnson County War: Also known as the War on Powder River and the Wyoming Range War, was a series of range conflicts that took place in Johnson, Wyoming between 1889 and 1893. The conflicts started when cattle companies ruthlessly persecuted supposed rustlers throughout the grazing lands of Wyoming. As tensions swelled between the large established ranchers and the smaller settlers in the state, violence finally culminated in Powder River Country, when the former hired armed gunmen to invade the country and wipe out the competition. When word came out of the gunmen's initial incursion into the territory, the small-time farmers and ranchers, as well as the state lawmen, formed a posse of 200 men to fight them back which led to a grueling stand-off. The war ended when the United States Cavalry, on the orders of President Benjamin Harrison, relieved the two forces, and the failure to convict the invaders of the murders they had committed.

The events have since become a highly mythologized and symbolic story of the Wild West, and over the years, variations of the storyline have come to include some of its most famous historical figures. Its themes and elements of class warfare have served as a classical basis for numerous popular novels, films, and television shows of the Western genre, as well as being one of the most well-known range wars of the American frontier.

- Frank M. Canton: Josiah Horner (September 15, 1849 – September 27, 1927), better known as Frank M. Canton, was a famous American Old West lawman, gunslinger, cowboy and at one point in his life, an outlaw.

- Jim Averell: An alleged Wyoming cattle rustler. They hung Averell along with "Cattle Kate" Watson by a cattle baron faction in 1889, just one of the many incidents that led to the Johnson County War.

- Ellen Liddy Watson (July 2, 1860 – July 20, 1889) was a pioneer of Wyoming who became erroneously known as Cattle Kate, a post claimed outlaw of the Old West. The "outlaw" characterization is a dubious one, as she was not violent and was never charged with any crime during her life. Accused of cattle rustling, she was ultimately lynched by agents of powerful cattle ranchers as an example of what happens to those who opposed them or who threatened their interests. Her life has become an Old West legend.

- Belinda Mulrooney: (1872–1967) was an entrepreneur and purportedly the "richest woman in the Klondike". She made one fortune in the Klondike Gold Rush, lost it, and amassed a second, which lasted most of her life.

- Wovoka: (c. 1856 - September 20, 1932), also known as Jack Wilson, was the Northern Paiute religious leader who founded the Ghost Dance movement. Wovoka means "cutter" or "woodcutter" in the Northern Paiute language.

- Ghost Dance Movement: The Ghost Dance (Caddo: Nanissáanah, also called the Ghost Dance of 1890) was a new religious movement incorporated into numerous Native American belief systems. According to the teachings of the Northern Paiute spiritual leader Wovoka (renamed Jack Wilson), proper practice of the dance would reunite the living with spirits of the dead. This dance would bring the spirits of the dead to fight on their behalf, make the white colonists leave, and bring peace, prosperity, and unity to native peoples throughout the region

- Quetzalcoatlus: /kɛtsəlkoʊˈætləs/ was a pterosaur known from the Late Cretaceous period of North

America (Maastrichtian stage) and the largest known member of the Azhdarchidae, a family of advanced toothless pterosaurs with unusually long, stiffened necks. Its name comes from the Mesoamerican feathered serpent god Quetzalcoatl.

- General George Custer: George Custer was an American military commander and brevet general who in 1876 led 210 men into battle at Little Bighorn against Native Americans. Custer and his men were killed.

Chapter 5
Westward Ho

As Laz fell back into his train seat, he breathed a huge sigh of relief and exhaustion. So much had happened in just the last few days that he felt bone weary right down to the bottom of his clawed feet. He thought he could sleep for a week.

He arranged his tail into the seat, which had been designed more for human posteriors. As he relaxed back and closed his eyes, he felt a huge thud!

A short, stocky human fireplug had flopped down and engulfed the seat right next to him. It almost felt as if the train had hit something solid while rolling out of the station.

Laz was just getting ready to yell "Hey get the heck off me and find another seat!"! The human bowling ball looked over with the most disarming smile Laz had ever seen, and said in a deep rich voice right out of an Italian opera; "Hello there Mr. Lézard! My name is Bartholomew Bettus. You may call me Bart. I bet on everything, and I have decided to bet on you!!!"

This was the oddest thing anyone had ever said to Laz. He would have fallen right out of his seat if there had been any room left to do so.

Laz puffed up his green cheeks and exclaimed, "Mr. Buttabetus what the heck are you talking about!!!"

Bart just smiled; "It is Bartholomew Bettus! Just call me Bart. I found the news article about you to be the most compelling bit of reading I have ever had the fortune to run across. I am a writer, unfortunately, with just a tiny tad of writer's block going on right now. I have decided that you need to have your story told. I have also decided to be the one to tell it. Now don't thank me. It is my pleasure!"

Laz was trying to wiggle out of his seat and get as far away from this odd human as he possibly could.

Bart said; "Now Mr. Lézard again there is no need to jump up and thank me. Just relax and let's discuss the adventure that we are embarking upon together. I may be a little overqualified to offer my assistance to you, for free, but I have this gut feeling that you are headed for greatness."

Laz stopped fighting Bart's bodily form of capture for just a moment. It was hard to fight back against Bart's strange off the wall logic. There was something in the voice and the powerful shoulders and arms that made Laz feel squished, but it also felt oddly safe.

There may have been no reason to do so, but Laz felt himself willing to hear more from this strange human! He said; "Now why in the world should I trust you?"

Bart looked at him as if this was the silliest question he had ever heard; "Why because I am here! Where you are going, you will need all the help you can get!!!"

Lazarus threw up his arms and said; "Well then you may as well call me Laz!"

"OK, Laz it is then, by golly!"

"So anyway Laz I had already been considering a trip to the Gold Rush when I read your story in the paper yesterday. It hit me like a ton of bricks, and I made my decision right there on the spot, I tell you!"

"I said to myself; 'By golly Bart, this Mr. Lézard fellow is going to need your help. He is going to need a sidekick to smooth out the rough spots in the road."

Laz thought to himself; 'This guy sure has a funny way of talking. If nothing else I could use him as a rolling pin to smooth out those rough spots.'

As the train picked up steam so did Bart. He had plans and ideas for everything that lay ahead. He was a ball of energy. As it turned out Bart, together with reporter Ed Towse, had already made plans. They convinced the owner of the Cheyenne Daily Sun to finance Bart's trip to get Laz's story first hand. The people of Cheyenne were intrigued by Lazarus Lézard, and they wanted to hear more.

Laz was amazed that Bart could have accomplished all this in just a couple of days.

The train rolled west with Bart talking nonstop about all the adventures that lay ahead.

Chapter 6
San Francisco or Bust

The first thing Laz and Bart did was upgrade their tickets to a private sleeper car. Split two ways it was the smart move.

Laz had to remind Bart that it was called a *Sleeper Car* as Bart would have talked nonstop around the clock.

The train was passing through some beautiful and interesting country. In Wyoming, they went through cowboy towns such as

Laramie, Rawlins, and Bitter Creek. They could see waterways teeming with wildlife. Everywhere they looked there were mountains and valleys with Eagles and many other species of birds in the air.

In Utah, they actually passed near the Great Salt Lake. The train had stopped in Ogden, Utah where many people got off heading to Salt Lake City.

The train next moved into Nevada heading for a stop in Reno. Bart had many stories to tell about the wild days of Virginia City that was high up in the mountains above Reno. It was another wild and crazy mining town. He pointed out men who could be gamblers judging by their talk and the way they dressed. The gamblers were more than likely heading for the gaming tables of Casinos like the famous Bucket of Blood that gave Virginia City the feeling of danger and excitement.

This really piqued Laz's interest. Bart said; "Don't you worry my thick skinned comrade, you're not missing anything. Where we are headed the *Bucket of Blood will look like a children's schoolyard."

The last leg of the train trip went from Reno through the mountains and ended in San Francisco.

Bart and Laz had several days to kill until they were to take a steamship from there to Seattle, Washington. Bart had spent a lot of time in San Francisco, and he was looking forward to showing Laz the sights.

There was great food to be had and Bart knew all the best spots to get it. Fresh seafood at the future home of Fisherman's Landing and chop suey in Chinatown was just the first day.

Policeman that Ran Off to Join the Circus?:

Jesse B. Cook (1860-1938)

Bart contacted his friend *Jesse Brown Cook, who was a San Francisco, police officer. Jesse would later become Chief of Police and Police Commissioner.

It seemed Lazarus' story had already spread in some local circles, and Jesse wanted to meet him.

At this time, Officer Cook was a sergeant in the Chinatown squad, and he had many wild stories to tell of early San Francisco history. He had dealt with bad problems such as the *Tong Wars over his years there.

Laz had his stories about the Tongs as well.

Note: See Book 2 of the Lézard Family Chronicles.

Chinese businessmen had set up the Tongs as their form of protection from other gangs that were demanding protection money and stealing from them.

The Chinese were a quiet, humble and hardworking people that had come to the United States to work on the building of the rail systems across the country. They had also found work in mining and the Gold Rush at Sutter's Mill in California.

As happened with many large communities in the Wild West, San Francisco had its gambling dens, saloons, houses of ill-repute and drug problems. Chinatown was no exception. It had its Sex Slaves and Opium Dens.

The Tongs became a bigger problem for the businessmen than what they had been organized to cure.

This was still several years before the *Great San Francisco Earthquake that broke the back of the Tongs.

Officer Cook and the rest of the Police Department still had their hands full on many levels.

Because of his help with the train robbery, the police department made Laz an honorary member of the San Francisco police department.

He was amazed and slightly embarrassed by the attention he was getting for just helping his friend keep from getting shot in the back.

After all the years of prejudice he had suffered he did not totally hate the attention he was getting. Bart got a big kick out of Laz's discomfort with his newfound fame.

Laz found his new friend Jesse Brown Cook fascinating. His past was really interesting and hit very close to home for Lazarus.

Before he joined the police department he had studied taxidermy, worked as a sailor, drayman, and butcher. He even toured Europe as a contortionist in a traveling circus.

Jesse could bend his body into all types of positions like a human pretzel. The Chinese people he interacted with found this peculiar policeman of great interest, and they held him in high esteem in their community.

Jesse's police career began in San Antonio, Texas, and he was also a police officer in San Diego before he returned to San Francisco.

Being also from Europe and having his own background with the circus Lazarus and Jesse became fast friends and would work together on some cases in Laz's future.

A Kaleidoscope of Contacts:

Laz was thrilled with all his new friends. An Indian Medicine Man that was an amateur magician, a sheriff that rode down crooks while jumping from trains on his horse, a San Francisco police officer that ran off to Europe to join a circus as a young man, and, of course, Bart, who seemed to know everyone on earth.

He couldn't forget his friends Sebastiano and Joseph Salerno, who had started Little Italy in Omaha.

What could possibly be next?

*Chapter 6 Endnotes:

- **The Bucket of Blood Saloon:** VIRGINIA CITY, NEVADA-- The Bucket of Blood Saloon, was rebuilt after the fire of 1875. In spite of its sinister name, the Saloon today gives off the charm of the old time hey-days with its many hanging lamps and mirrors. Memories of the past await the visitor wandering into the bar for a cold drink in this cool oasis.

Note: Author Don Parent went there in 1957 with his family. He was 12 years old. He found Silver Dollars left in some of the slot machines and on the floor. They still used them back then. He wishes he still had them today!

- Jesse Brown Cook: (1860-1938) began his career in the San Francisco Police Department as a beat officer, and later served as a sergeant of the "Chinatown Squad." He served as Chief of Police after the 1906 earthquake, retired, and was later appointed to the Police Commission.

  His police career began in San Antonio, Texas, and was a police officer in San Diego before he returned to San Francisco.

  Cook collected extensive photographs, clippings and ephemera relating to the Police Department, San Francisco and the surrounding area, now in the Bancroft Library.

  Cook described San Francisco's Chinatown in the *San Francisco Police and Peace Officers' Journal* issue of June 1931.

- Tong Wars: The Tong Wars were a series of violent disputes fought from the 1880s through 1921 among rival Chinese Tong factions centered in San Francisco's Chinatown district. Tong wars could be triggered by a variety of inter-gang grievances, from the public besmirching of another tong's honor to failure to make full payment for a "slave girl" to the murder of a rival tong member. Each Tong had salaried soldiers, known as Boo How Doy, who fought in Chinatown alleys and streets over the control of

opium, prostitution, gambling, and territory.
It was the San Francisco earthquake of 1906 and
subsequent fires, caused by the giant earthquake
that was the death knell for the Tongs at least in
San Francisco. It destroyed the brothels, gambling
dens, and opium houses that the criminal
organizations had used for the majority of their
revenue.

- **The San Francisco Earthquake:**
On the morning of April 18, 1906, a massive earthquake shook San Francisco,

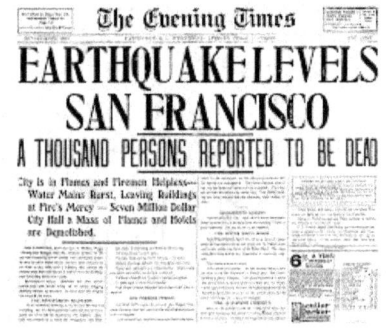

California. Though the quake lasted less than a
minute, its immediate impact was disastrous. The
earthquake also ignited several fires around the
city that burned for three days and destroyed
nearly 500 city blocks.

Despite a quick response from San Francisco's
large military population, the city was devastated.
The earthquake and fires killed an estimated 3,000
people and left half of the city's 400,000 residents
homeless. Aid poured in from around the country
and the world, but those who survived faced
weeks of difficulty and hardship.

Being a shipping port, fishing village and
transportation hub early San Francisco had its
share of problems and wild times, to say the least.

Chapter 7
Steaming North

Lazarus and Bart arranged passage to Seattle with the Pacific Coast Steamship Company. Their days on board were amazing with views of the gorgeous coastlines of California, Oregon, and Washington.

They passed many fishing boats spreading their nets, lumber companies working the coastal forests and huge schools of porpoise that loved to follow the ship as if playing with it. The sight of whales would have passengers rushing to the rail for a look.

The deckhands pointed out giant schools of tuna and other large fish feeding off in the distance. The schools could be spotted by the flocks of seabirds fighting and diving for any leftovers flopping at the surface.

After being stuck in train cars for so long, the openness and sea air were liberating. Laz even got Bart to do some serious exercise walking circuits on the decks and other forms of aerobics. He started teaching Bart and some of the deck hands Kung Fu moves. Other passengers watched in fascination as Lazarus spun, kicked and lashed out with tail whips. This upset Bart no end as he lacked in the tail department.

Bart was a surprisingly quick learner however and extremely strong. He was much more limber than his body shape would have suggested.

The ship stayed two nights in Seattle, which gave Laz and Bart time for meetings with Allen Derby, the Dawson, company representative.

They had a million questions for him, and it was a very informative two days. Of course, Bart had a ton of Seattle food and drink questions and made a list of the best breakfast, lunch, and dinner choices available over the next couple of days.

The ship headed north with stops along the way to their final destination. That was the continent's northernmost deep-water seaport of Skagway.

The sights and sounds kept getting better. As they looked toward the distant shores, they saw vistas of powerful snow covered mountains. The peaks were home to bald eagles and the waterways were filled with killer whales, sea lions and hundreds of the smaller seals swimming and crawling up onto rocky beaches and even floating chunks of ice.

The distance was a 1000 mile trip by the sea so they were able to get lots of exercise in along the way. They knew that they would have to be strong for the strenuous travel ahead once they landed in Skagway.

Skagway:

Their first view of the harbor was shocking, to say the least. They had expected to see a quiet small town with not much going on.

What they came into was an extremely congested harbor with all types of boats fighting for room to offload the hopeful miners and their mountains of supplies.

The action was intense. It was surprising that more accidents didn't happen to spill bodies and cargo into the freezing churning ocean. At these temperatures death would come quickly from the jagged ice and frigid saltwater swirling in the murky depths. The froth on the Whitecaps mirrored the tips of the surrounding snowcapped mountains. It was hard to believe this was supposed to be the summer months.

The new arrivals had to anchor up to a mile offshore. Overloaded scows were shuttling men, women, and even children, and their provisions to the town's gravel beach.

On the beach, owners protected their piles of belongings with scattershot curses and the rapid cocking of pistols. It was pure mayhem at its most deadly pace.

The slopes above the beach were filled with tents and rickety wooden shacks that looked like they were ready to fall down of their own volition. The strong north winds did not help this situation at all.

Skagway's original Inuit name Skaguay meant "A Windy Place with White Caps on the Water."

When Skaguay put in for its own post office, a Washington bureaucrat thought they must have spelled it wrong on the forms and changed it to Skagway.

There were over 4000 people fighting for whatever type of business they thought they could make a buck at.

There were even a couple of churches hastily thrown up. Judging by the look of many of the other businesses the town could have used a few more Godly places.

Over the next few years, tens of thousands more would land at either Skagway or the neighboring hamlet of Dyea.

After Lazarus had reached the shore, he needed to find the post office. The travel package that he had received from Alan Derby had told him to look up *Clara Richards, who had just been named the first Postmaster for the area by President McKinley. Her brother Arthur was appointed Deputy Marshal. They handled both Skagway and tiny Dyea.

There were two parallel passes from the coastline through the mountains into the interior. Out of Skagway the Stampeders, as the gold-crazed hopefuls became known, could take the White Pass. Also, Skagway had the deeper harbor, so most boats offloaded there.

*Dyea developed because it was at the foot of the Chilkoot Pass which was considered a little easier to traverse. Now that didn't mean easy by any stretch of the imagination. They were both incredibly hard especially when you factor in the many trips the Stampeders had to make to get all their provisions across. Many people died along with their pack animals. Much of the time they could not be used at all. There were not many animals available, and some ended up as food. There were no restaurants or stores along the way.

Luckily for Lazarus and Bart they had a professional contact in Skagway. There were many crooks and conmen working their schemes on the unsuspecting marks.

One such crook and major con man was Jefferson

Randolph "Soapy Smith. Before he came to Skagway Smith earned his nickname "Soapy" with a more conventional confidence game.

Traveling around the Southwest, Smith would briefly set up shop in the street selling bars of soap wrapped in blue tissue paper. He promised the naive crowds that a few lucky purchasers would find a $100 bill wrapped inside a few of the $5 bars of soap. Inevitably, one of the first to buy a bar would shout with pleasure and happily display a genuine $100 bill. Sales were brisk after that. The lucky purchaser, of course, was a plant by Soapy

Once he arrived in Dyea Soapy, set up a telegraph office. The homesick Stampeders paid big bucks to send messages home. What they didn't realize was that the telegraph wires ended a few hundred yards behind the building.

It is little wonder that a disgruntled engineer put an end to Soapy in a shootout at a town meeting. Laz and Bart had landed in the wild frontier, to say the least.

Post Mistress Clara Richards and her brothers proved to be a huge help to them. They had tons of important information to share with Laz and Bart. For one thing, they were fortunate to be making the trip during the start of the warmer months. Many people had died by being frozen in for months on the trail.

The Stampeders were legally required to carry not only their mining gear but also one year's food and provisions per person. This requirement made their travel extremely rigorous and exhausting. As hard as it is to imagine some single women with the lure of riches or rich husbands made the trip. Some of them proved tougher than the men they passed on the way over the rugged trails.

Because Lazarus had a job waiting for him, he and Bart did not need the heavy equipment or the provisions other than what they would use on the trail.

Laz's provisions, which would get him to Dawson, were already waiting for him. Thank the Good Lord he didn't need to haul a year's supplies. Clara took them shopping for Bart's needs. She did not want to see him get ripped off and pay too much. Bart had thought ahead and brought many items of canned and dry goods, a good backpack and plenty of his favorite cigars and cognac.

After much back and forth they decided to use the Chilkoot Pass route. Clara took them by wagon over to her office in Dyea.

Several days later it was time to hit the trail. One thing they were thankful for was the good hiking boots that they had been smart enough to break in along the way. They had worn them on many of their exercise walks on their ship's deck to get them ready.

Laz had brought plenty of specially made socks and gloves that could handle his claws. Bart almost fell laughing the first time he saw Lazarus in his specially made long johns. "Lazarus, my boy, you make quite the fashion statement! Wait right there while I set up my camera."

"Just try it, Bart! You'll look just as funny with the tripod sticking out of the seat of your pants!!!"

After the goodbyes to Clara and her brothers they moved out. They had been set up with a good guide that would help them pack their provisions over the pass. They would only need to go over once which turned out to be a gift from Heaven. That one trip made them wonder how anyone could be so hungry for gold that they would make the trip six or more times to move their provisions across.

Hiking past the decomposing bodies of dead horses and mules was bad enough. The guide pointed to places where men and women had died trying to make the treacherous trip as well. Down in steep crevasses, they could see rusting equipment that fell in along with the person or animal that was carrying it.

Just up ahead they saw something that brought a cheer from their lips. They were excited to reach the summit. The happiness did not last once they started heading down the other slippery slope. The downgrade rapidly proved to be just as miserable. Slipping and sliding in mud, with heavy packs on their backs, was extremely scary and hard on the legs and bodies. Laz had an advantage in that he could use his tail for balance and leverage. If it hadn't been so cold, he would have pulled off his gloves and boots to bring his claws into play as well. The trek was a cold, miserable, hell on earth.

Finally, after a hike that was torture on their minds and bodies, they spotted Lake Lindeman in the distance. This sight almost brought tears to their eyes. Their guide had made arrangements for them to travel down the Yukon River by boat.

The boat they were to board was not so much a boat as it was a floating river raft. It did not look as seaworthy as the ships they had been on over the past weeks, but anything was better than what they had just gone through on foot.

The thought of riding a craft like this for 550 miles downriver to Dawson was a little worrisome. Granted it was a very large heavy duty raft with a railing around it. But it was still a raft. It had a long tiller sticking out the rear, and there was a large shack built topside.

The raft was loaded with supplies. They were surprised to see so many people that the company also had hired. This craft belonged to the company. They had been hiring many people. Lazarus wondered how many the company had shanghaied in much the same way he was?

Because of the huge influx of so many stampeders, Dawson needed to bring in many other trades. The rapid expansion of the town had need of many types of workers. Many of these ended up with their personal version of gold fever. They snuck off into the hills themselves.

The Dawson Town Council worked with the company that had hired Lazarus and all the others. As the population of Dawson exploded they had reached out to large towns like New York to find suitably trained individuals to help support it. All the newcomers had signed contracts, but that did not stop some from going AWOL with a pick, shovel, and gold pan, to try their luck at finding the Mother Lode!

*Chapter 7 Endnotes:

- Clara Richards: The first Postmaster (then called Postmistress) was appointed in the 1890s in Dyea by President McKinley. That curiously was a 51- year-old woman who came up to Alaska from Boise, Idaho. Clara and her brothers Daniel and Arthur Allen Richards were from a large family. The 8 kids were all born in Middleburg, Ohio to their farmer father and mother, but they had moved to Idaho sometime in the late 1800's. When the three siblings got to Dyea, Arthur Allen was appointed Deputy Marshal, and Daniel was involved in some business.

The real story here was the scandal involving the Dyea post office. While Clara no doubt was working as hard as she could, the post office was a 14X20 cabin that by all accounts was deplorable. On most days the line stretched far and away with 300-400 men hoping to send and receive mail. Clara's rule was that no man could ask for mail for any more that 2 people. So if a guy came down to get mail for his companions, it would take him all day. The amount of mail going north from Seattle was stupendous: Eight steamers full per month docked in Dyea. One steamer alone carried 4000 pieces of mail.

- Jefferson Randolph "Soapy" Smith: (November 2, 1860 – July 8, 1898) was a con artist, saloon and gambling house proprietor, gangster, and crime boss of the 19th-century Old West. His most famous scam was the$100 dollar bill in the soap

package presented him with the sobriquet of "Soapy", which remained with him until his death.
Although he traveled and operated his confidence swindles all across the western United States, he is most famous for having a major hand in the organized criminal operations of Denver and Creede, Colorado, and Skagway, Alaska, from 1879 to 1898. In Denver, he ran several saloons, gambling halls, cigar stores, and auction houses that specialized in cheating their clientele. In Denver, Soapy began to make a name for himself across the country as a bad man. Denver is also where he entered the arena of political fixing, where, for favors, he could sway the outcome of city, county, and state elections.

He used the same methods of operation when he settled in the towns of Creede and Skagway, opening businesses with the primary goal of gently robbing his customers while making a name for himself. He died in spectacular fashion in the shootout on Juneau Wharf in Skagway.

- **Dyea** (/daɪˈiː/ *dye-EE*) is a former town in the U.S. state of Alaska. A few people live on individual small homesteads in the valley; however, it is largely abandoned. It is located at the convergence of the Taiya River and Taiya Inlet on the south side of the Chilkoot Pass within the limits of the Municipality of Skagway Borough, Alaska.

During the Klondike Gold Rush, prospectors disembarked at its port and used the Chilkoot Trail, a Tlingit trade route over the Coast Mountains, to begin their journey to the gold fields around Dawson City, Yukon, about 800 km (500 mi) away. Confidence man and crime boss Soapy Smith, famous for his underworld control of the neighboring town of Skagway in 1897-98 is believed to have had control of Dyea as well.

The port at Dyea had shallow water while neighboring Skagway had deep water. They abandoned Dyea when the White Pass and Yukon Route railroad chose the White Pass Trail (instead of the alternative Chilkoot Trail), which began at Skagway, for its route.

Chilkoot Trail and Dyea Site is a U.S. National Historic Landmark.

Dyea is now within the Klondike Gold Rush National Historical Park. All that remains are some foundations surrounded by scraps of lumber and metal, three cemeteries, including one where almost every person buried died on the same date in an avalanche on the gold rush trail, and the ruins of the wharf. Visitors can usually spot brown bears, black bears, caribou, and eagles. Brown bears tend to use the Dyea inlets to feed during salmon spawning season (July–August).

Chapter 8
Down the Crazy River

The first leg of the river trip was about 90 miles down to the new town of Whitehorse. After the horrors of the Chilkoot Pass, this river ride was a giant relief. The only thing that concerned Lazarus was the many bear sightings along the way.

The Bears were not at all interested in lizard meat, however. They were too busy ripping huge king salmon from the cold water with their giant claws. They had plenty of the delicious red meat the salmon were famous for.

The Captain and crew of their boat actually had plenty of it for sale themselves. The passengers could buy it fresh, dried or smoked. This made Bart extremely happy, and he took full advantage of it. Being able to stuff their packs with the smoked and dried salmon assured them that they would not go hungry on the trip ahead.

As they came upon the area known as *Whitehorse, the Captain and crew poled the craft to shore.

Whitehorse was named for the historic rapids on the Yukon River there. The water roiling over the large boulders resembled the flowing manes of charging white horses. With very little imagination you could see the

heads of beautiful stallions racing full speed over and around the rocks.

The Stampeders had to bypass this treacherous stretch of water of Miles Canyon and Whitehorse Rapids, south of the present-day city.

They offloaded the raft on the shore. The passengers had to wait overnight for wagons to return to move them and their supplies around the rapids. Some enterprising business pioneers had set up a camp with a saloon and hotel. They had built a road to ferry travelers around the rough water area.

Minus the passengers and all of their equipment the crew could then fight the rapids to meet them down the river at the other side.

Old Friends Meet Again:

That night as they sat in the saloon they heard a booming voice from across the room; ***"Bart Bettus, you old son of a gun!!!"***

Bart stood up and was engulfed in a huge bear hug. He leaned back and exclaimed; "Alexander! By golly! What the heck are you doing out in this crazy place?"

Lazarus sat there stupefied by the sight of these two Grizzly bears jumping around and beating each other on the back.

They finally calmed down, and Alexander noticed the strange looking lizard sitting at Bart's table.

"And what have we here Bart?" He exclaimed. "If you aren't the first Lizard I have ever seen all wrapped up to handle the snow! Now there has to be one heck of a story in this!"

Bart said, "Lazarus let me introduce you to this crazy Greek Buffoon! This is my friend *Alexander Pantages. Alex this is the soon to be famous Lazarus Lézard!"

Alex gazed at Laz with an appraising look and asked; "What do you mean by famous Bart?"

" Well By Golly I'm on my way to Dawson with Mr. Honorary Deputy Sheriff Lézard here. I am going to write his story!" He then went on to relate the whole attempted train robbery.

Bart exclaimed; "I want to tell you my friend Lazarus Lézard here is a bonafide hero, by Golly!!!"

Alex sat back with an interested look on his face; "You know, you two, I think I did hear a little about this when I was in Seattle last week. Well Mr. Lézard, let me tip my hat to you."

"I am also on my way to Dawson. It looks like we may be on the same river ride tomorrow. This will give us plenty of time to catch up since I saw you last Bart."

"So tell me, Alex, what in the heck are you doing way out here?" And off the stories went. If anything Alex could out-talk Bart. Laz just sat back with a smile and listened to some amazing stories between these two old friends. With snifters of brandy and cigar smoke haze, they talked far into the wee hours of the night.

Alexander had quite a storied past indeed: He had been born in Greece. When he was just nine years old, his father took Alexander on a business trip to Cairo in Egypt. Alexander did not want to go back to Greece, so he decided to run away. He never set foot in Greece again.

He then went to sea and spent the next two years working as a deckhand. He got off a ship in Panama to work on the Panama Canal. While there he came down with malaria. He was warned by doctors to move to cooler climates to battle the illness.

He headed north, eventually settling in San Francisco where he worked as a waiter and also, briefly and unsuccessfully, as a boxer.

He was on his way to the Klondike Gold Rush when he ran into Bart and Lazarus. In the future, his name Pantages would be synonymous with the theaters he built all over the United States and Canada.

Once in Dawson, he would become the business partner and boyfriend of famous Saloon owner *Klondike Kate" Rockwell.

He opened his first theater, "The Orpheus" there.

Chapter 8 Endnotes:

- Whitehorse: total area population 27,889 as of 2013 is the capital and largest city of Yukon, Canada and the largest city in Northern Canada. It was incorporated in 1950 and is located at kilometer 1426 on the Alaska Highway in southern Yukon. Whitehorse's downtown and Riverdale areas occupy both shores of the Yukon River, which originates in British Columbia and meets the Bering Sea in Alaska. The city was named after the White Horse Rapids for their resemblance to the mane of a white horse, near Miles Canyon before the river was dammed. Because of the city's location in the Whitehorse valley, the climate is milder than other comparable northern communities such as Yellowknife. At this latitude winter days were short and summer days have 20 hours of daylight. Whitehorse, as reported by Guinness World Records, is the city with the least air pollution in the world.

- Alexander Pantages: (1867 – February 17, 1936) was a Greek American vaudeville and early motion picture producer and impresario who created a large and powerful circuit of theaters across the western United States and Canada. At the height of his empire, he

ALEXANDER PANTAGES

owned or operated 84 theaters across the United States and Canada. His first showplaces were in the Klondike with his then girlfriend, Klondike Kate.

- "Klondike Kate" Rockwell:

   Kathleen Eloise Rockwell (1873–1957), was best known as "Klondike Kate", and later known as Kate Rockwell Warner Matson Van Duren. She gained her fame as a dancer and vaudeville star during the Klondike Gold Rush, where she met Alexander Pantages, who later became a very successful vaudeville/motion picture mogul. She gained notoriety for her flirtatious dancing and ability to keep hard-working miners happy if not inebriated. She died in obscurity after some minor success training Hollywood starlets in the 1940s.

Chapter 9
On to Dawson City

The next morning Lazarus, Bart, and Alexander loaded their gear onto one of the wagons to head further downstream past the rapids.

Lazarus was amazed at how they could wake up so refreshed after drinking and smoking so many cigars while he felt a little greener around the gills himself!

While on the wagons they had sightings through the trees of other rafts and boats rocking and rolling in and around huge boulders and scary drops into the churning water.

Bart said; "The next time I make this river trip I will pay extra to be allowed to shoot the rapids with the crew, by golly!!!"

Once below the worst of the rapids they then loaded back onto the huge raft that looked no worse for wear after shooting the white water.

The next leg of the trip to Dawson was still hundreds of miles but due to the long summer days in this part of the world, they could travel close to 18 hours in daylight.

Amazingly further north at their destination of Dawson, there could be over 20 hours of daylight during the month of June.

Of course, the opposite was true during the freezing winter months.

All those long days and nights made for some really interesting and even strange happenings:

The Cremation of Sam McGee
There are strange things done in the midnight sun

By the men who moil for gold
The Arctic trails have their secret tales
That would make your blood run cold;
The Northern Lights have seen queer sights,
But the queerest they ever did see
Was that night on the marge of *Lake Lebarge
I cremated Sam McGee.
By Robert Wm. Service (1874-1958)

After heading further toward Dawson, they traversed Lake Lebarge, which even at the start of the summer months could have crazy weather that could cause havoc on travel and tempers.

Long Days and Long Nights:

Another strange thing caused by Long Days was the mega size veggies they could grow at places like White Horse and also in Dawson. Any land that saw good sunlight was at a premium.

During his studies, before the trip, Lazarus had learned that they could grow amazing vegetables in Dawson. With so many hours of sunlight, the vegetables grew to huge sizes. They could grow carrots as big as your arm and cabbage larger than a big pumpkin.

Hunting, Fishing, and Canning:

The opposite was also true during the dark winter months. Everyone with any sense spent most of the long sunlit days canning, drying, and freezing anything they could shoot, hook, or grow.

Hanky Panky:

The long nights of winter had their own dark stories as well. The saloons and houses of ill repute did their most rollicking business during these months. In the daylight months, the miners were all at their claims working as many of the daylight

hours as their bodies could handle. There was no energy left for any hanky-panky or drunken card games.

During the dark, freezing days of winter cabin, fever saw many gunfights break out over crooked card games or jealousy over the few women available.

Past Lake Laberge and on to Dawson:

This 400-mile trip could be over two weeks depending on weather conditions. Even in summer it could be very cold, and storms would pop up out of nowhere and last for hours or days.

The crew ran fishing lines behind the raft. Dark shiny pieces of metal with a hook behind it seemed to work well for catching pike, grayling, and salmon.

Watching the fishing line zing and go rigid became a fun pastime as the days stretched into weeks. The passengers even started making bets on what kind of fish would be caught next. They also bet on how many bears would be sighted during a four hour period. They made games out of anything and everything that would pass the time for them. There was always a card game going on.

Over the many days to come on the water, with little else to do, the passengers had endless questions to ask the captain and crew about conditions in their new upcoming home.

The crew tried to spin a positive future for them, but it became quite clear that only the strong could survive for any length of time in the hostile land they were heading toward.

The ones, like Lazarus, who had jobs waiting, had a better potential for success in what lay ahead.

There were still some people on the raft that were strictly going for the gold. The closer the river took them toward Dawson, the wilder their dreams of riches became.

They had visions of taking their millions home to build mansions and open all sorts of wild business ventures as if the one that lay just ahead wasn't wild enough for them.

There were others going for their own reasons like Bart and Alexander. Alex knew that there was a far better chance to do well by bringing entertainment to the area.

Bart, who made friends with everyone, spent a lot of time talking with a fellow writer. Jack was a young struggling writer that was also looking for inspiration in the rugged wilderness of the gold fields. Like Bart, he felt there would be many exciting things to write about.

Jack had been born in San Francisco, California. He  worked at various hard labor jobs. He pirated for oysters on San Francisco Bay, served on a fish patrol to capture poachers, sailed the Pacific on a sealing ship, and joined Kelly's Army of the unemployed working men. He hoboed around the country and then returned to attend high school at age 19.

Always a prolific reader, he consciously chose to become a writer to escape from the horrific prospects of life as a factory worker. He studied other writers and began to submit stories, jokes, and poems to various publications, mostly without success.

The three friends took him under their wings and by the time they landed in Dawson their group of friends had grown a little larger.

The adventure writing ended up working very well for their new friend *Jack London. His books "Call of the Wild" and "White Fang" were just a few of his best sellers to come from his travels in the Yukon and other locations around the globe.

*Chapter 9 Endnotes:

- *Lake Laberge is a widening of the Yukon River north of Whitehorse, Yukon in Canada. It is fifty kilometers long and ranges from two to five kilometers wide. Its water is always very cold, and its weather often harsh and suddenly variable. The local Southern Tutchone called it Tàa'an Män, Tagish knew it as Kluk-tas-Si and the Tlingit as Tahini-wud.
Its English name comes from 1870 commemorating Michel LaBerge (1836–1909) - born in Chateauguay, Quebec, the first French-Canadian to explore the Yukon in 1866.[2] It was well-known to prospectors during the Klondike Gold Rush of the 1890s, as they would pass Lake Laberge on their way down the Yukon River to Dawson City. Jack London's Grit of Women (1900)

and The Call of the Wild (1903), and Robert W. Service's poem "The Cremation of Sam McGee" (1907) mention the lake.

- *John Griffith "Jack London (born John Griffith Chaney, January 12, 1876 – November 22, 1916) was an American author, journalist, and social activist. A pioneer in the then-burgeoning world of commercial magazine fiction, he was one of the first fiction writers to obtain worldwide celebrity and a large fortune from his fiction alone.
Some of his most famous works include The Call of the Wild and White Fang, both set in the Klondike Gold Rush, as well as the short stories "To Build a Fire", "An Odyssey of the North", and "Love of Life". He also wrote of the South Pacific in such stories as "The Pearls of Parlay" and "The Heathen", and of the San Francisco Bay area in The Sea Wolf.

Chapter 10
The Gold Fields

On the fifteenth day of their river trip from Whitehorse, they began spotting more boats and more humanity. Logging work was going on plus small fishing camps and homesteads were scattered along the banks of the river. They could see more and more instances of smoke coming from chimneys farther back in the tree line.

The sounds of sawing, hammering and construction reached their ears. Roads were being graded, and buildings were going up everywhere.

More boats were moving up and down the river. All along the last 400 miles they had spotted some river traffic but nothing like what they now experienced.

As they pulled closer to the town, they could see that Dawson was bustling with activity. From a distance, it looked like a human anthill. There were hundreds of boats loading and unloading people and supplies. The building construction was going on everywhere at a breakneck pace.

After unloading their gear and provisions, the four friends helped each other arrange a wagon to get them to their destinations.

Jack was going to work for the newspaper *The Midnight Sun and anyone else that would buy his stories. He had made arrangements to sleep next to the printing presses until he could find something more comfortable.

Alexander headed for the theaters in search of "Klondike Kate" Rockwell his future girlfriend and business partner. He had a letter of introduction from mutual friends in Seattle.

Lazarus and Bart asked for directions to locate Frenchie, Laz's new employer. Laz had expected to find a full-fledged post office. What he found was quite something else.

Dawson was in an interesting situation for mail having come into being due to the gold rush. Travel was also tricky as the guys had come to know well. To get there, most Americans went through Skagway and Dyea, which are a part of the United States. Just over the Mountain passes they were then in Canada.

Dawson, in Canada, was only about 60 miles from the Alaskan border of the United States.

In the 1890's this caused all types of headaches about who did what and where. Did the United States have authority or Canada? What made it confusing was the influx of so many thousands of *Gold Stampeders from all over the world.

They were starved for news and letters from home. Lazarus had been hired by a private company that had sprung into being to fill the void that had opened up due to the inability of the two governments to come to terms with the situation.

It seemed that the Judge that had sent Lazarus to Dawson had a personal interest in the area. His brother-in-law Jean- Paul Leblanc AKA-Frenchie, and the Judge owned the company.

Fast Money:

The whole gold rush had become infested with "Get Rich Quick Schemes". After some concern and talks with Bart, Laz came to the realization that things could be worse. The company was doing well, and Frenchie assured Laz that there was plenty of work, and he would get paid well.

The miners were willing to pay huge amounts to receive their copies of the local newspapers and any mail from home that could get through. Being paid in gold dust and nuggets opened up this whole new business venture. Without Frenchie's services, the miners would have to leave their claims and travel all the way into town to spend many hours waiting in huge lines to receive their mail or send a letter. Some individuals' stood in line for up to three days. The lines were that long. It was a nightmare.

The government welcomed Frenchie's company because it helped alleviate the incredible pressure that the mail situation was causing them. His partner the Judge swung a lot of weight even though he was all the way back in New York.

Lazarus received a room in the company owned a boarding house. It was big enough to move in another bed for Bart. He had taken on some work as a writer for the newspapers. Frenchie contracted with many of the papers. Getting the news out to the mines was a two-way street. The town folk wanted to hear everything that went on in the outback.

Chapter 11
Order Amongst Madness

Frenchie gave Lazarus a few days to acquaint himself with his new surroundings. Learning the lay of the land would be of great value for what lay ahead.

Lazarus didn't need to report for his new job and training until Wednesday. This gave Laz and Bart some time to check out their new town and the surrounding countryside.

Dawson was something amazing to see **"By Golly"** as Bart would exclaim each time they turned a corner. "Would you look at that **by golly**," Bart would yell out as he grabbed Laz by the shoulder! Lazarus couldn't help but laugh because he was completely amazed as well. "OK, By Golly, he laughed as he elbowed his friend in his ample ribs.

Bart had been around a long time, but even he had never seen activity on this level. Lazarus, who was new to any frontier, was completely knocked off his claws by what was going on.

Everything in the town seemed brand new. Of course, it was brand new! As people poured into the area, there was a huge demand for anything and everything that a person would need to survive in this hardscrabble land.

The shopping and provisioning stores were extremely busy. With so much traffic and the summer months of 22 hour shopping days, the snow and ice thoroughfares had turned into muddy bogs.

To be able to walk around in the muck the town had built raised wooden walkways. On Sundays, everyone was clean and fancy, at least above the waist. With knee boots, you could hopefully keep your socks partially mud free.

The crisp, clean air was exhilarating although it could be punctuated by pungent wisps of horse manure steaming up from the streets and the rich woody smell of log fires that seeped out of every home and building.

Everywhere they looked, while out in the countryside, Lazarus and Bart saw the backdrop of sawtooth mountain peaks shooting straight up into the sky. These peaks took the breath right out of everyone and anyone that could see past their nose or snout. Lazarus was mesmerized by these vistas. He felt extremely fortunate to witness all these new sights day after day.

Important People:

One of the first people Lazarus contacted was Belinda Mulrooney. He had heard about her while crossing the United States. She was a ball of fire and the person to contact if you needed to find anything from boots to backpacks, from shovels to snowshoes. Rather than dig for the gold she was making her fortune by supplying hard to get items. She was also getting ready to build

*The Grand Forks Hotel and had big plans for everything. She was on her way to becoming one of the richest most important people in the Klondike.

She knew right away that due to his job description as a dog sledding mail carrier he would be in contact with everyone and a magnet for all the local news, gossip, and goings on in the Yukon. She decided that he would prove to be a good friend to have.

Old Fish Camp:

Dawson City spread out at the point where the Klondike River flowed into the Yukon River. The site was used for thousands of years by the native people of the area as a large fish camp where Inuits from all over came, caught, and dried their catches. This cache would take them through the long winter nights. With the deep ice, they could also dig out frozen pits to lay up moose, and other large game.

Keeping the Peace:

During the height of the Klondike Gold Rush, Dawson

City itself had a population of roughly 16,000 and was the commercial center for a total mining population of 30,000 people. It had opera houses, fine hotels, stores, breweries, churches, and of course, lots of saloons and banks.

What was surprising was that even though there was activity everywhere, things seemed to run in an orderly fashion. The presence of a contingent of the North West Mounted Police kept things from getting too out of hand.

The red uniforms of the Mounties (later known as the Royal Canadian Mounted Police) stood out so well that they seemed to be everywhere. If a townsperson viewed the same Mountie five times in a single day his brain told him that he had seen a full contingent. The many sightings of the red jackets went a long way to keeping the peace.

Some years earlier during his travels, Bart had come to know a Canadian military man by the name of *Samuel Benfield Steele.

Samuel was now the head of the Mounties for the whole Yukon Territory. His influence in the area was powerful, and his honest hard work kept Dawson from turning into another Skagway where the US Government still hadn't exerted control over all the crooks and conmen that were preying on the unsuspecting suckers that poured through their clutches. That's not to say there weren't some rats in Dawson, but the difference was very noticeable to the friends. The crooks didn't last long and after several run-ins with the Mounties, they headed back to Skagway for easier pickings.

The River Bottom Brotherhood:

It amazed Laz that Bart knew so many people in so many places in their travels. Getting reacquainted with Officer Steel would prove quite a boon to their future trials and tribulations in their new stomping grounds.

Their second night in town Laz and Bart took off to meet up for dinner with their two River Run buddies Alex and Jack. They all had a lot of important information to pass back and forth amongst themselves. Their new town had many things to offer. The million tons of gold being extracted just added to the excitement!!!

Between the four of them, they had made excellent new contacts, and happily old friendships cropped up from some of their past lives as well. Dawson was a magnet for adventurers from all over the world. Many of them had found mutual adventures in the same crazy places. "Birds of a feather" did seem to flock together! Excitement pulled many of the same people together time and time again to try their luck in the wild and exciting new frontiers that cropped up.

They decided to name their new exclusive club "The River Bottom Brotherhood"! This dinner became the first of many weekly meetings over the next few years for the RBB.

Mysterious Medicine Men:

Another authority figure that helped keep order between the Native People of the area and the newcomers was a mysterious Indian named *Chief Isaac. He would disappear into the wilderness for long periods of time but when he reappeared he would draw all the *Trondek Hwech'in Tribe members together for hours of important life lessons and tales of his travels.

He would meet with Officer Steele and others of the town to mediate any problems that would arise between the miners and Indians. This land was his people's, but, unfortunately due to the gold the newcomers were here to stay.

"Trondek Hwech'in" means "People of the River." They are descendants of the Hän-speaking people who have lived along the Yukon River for many thousands of years. They traveled extensively throughout their traditional territory harvesting salmon from the Yukon River and caribou from the Forty Mile and Porcupine Herds. No, they didn't harvest porcupines! That was their name for one particularly large herd of caribou.

Moose, small game, and a variety of plants and berries provided additional food sources. They were able to procure all the other raw materials needed to make tools, clothing and shelter from this diverse and rich environment. The Han traded with neighboring First Nations people and maintained interrelations through family connections and frequent gatherings.

Chief Isaac was not his Tribal name, but it was what he was known as in the Klondike. The natives and newcomers all treated him with great respect. He always seemed to have important deeper knowledge of mysteries that he hinted at but kept percolating just below the surface.

Chapter 11 Endnotes:

- The Grand Forks Hotel: In 1897 large amounts of gold were discovered in the Yukon, prompting huge numbers of prospectors to travel to the remote region, an event known as the Klondike Gold Rush. Belinda Mulrooney, a small-time businesswoman, arrived in Dawson City that year, intending to import goods and establish her enterprises. She established a restaurant and a shop in the city. She did a great business building homes for the immigrant prospectors. Mulrooney began to investigate other opportunities outside Dawson City. She researched along the creeks where the gold was being mined and decided that the spot where the Eldorado Creek met the Bonanza Creek would be an ideal place for a roadhouse hotel.

- Samuel Benfield Steele: Major General Sir Samuel Benfield Steele, KCMG, CB, MVO (5 January 1848 – 30 January 1919) was a distinguished Canadian soldier and police official. He was an officer of the North-West Mounted Police, most famously as head of the Yukon detachment during the Klondike Gold Rush, and commanding officer of Strathcona's Horse during the Boer War.

- Chief Isaac: Was the well-known chief of the Tr'ondëk Hwëch'in (Han) during the Klondike Goldrush of 1896 that resulted in the influx of thousands to their homeland. The Tr'ondëk Hwëch'in or People of the River is a small first nations group at Dawson City, Yukon at the confluence of the Klondike and Yukon Rivers.

- The Tr'ondëk Hwëch'in Tribe: ([tʼoⁿdək hwətʃʼin]; formerly the Dawson Indian Band) is a First Nation band government located in the Canadian territory, Yukon. Its main population center is

Dawson City, Yukon.
Many of today's Tr'ondëk Hwëch'in, or people of the river, are descendants of the Hän-speaking people who have lived along the Yukon River for thousands of years. They traveled extensively throughout their traditional territory harvesting salmon from the Yukon River and caribou from the Fortymile and Porcupine Herds. Moose, small game, and a variety of plants and berries provided additional food sources. Other raw materials needed to make tools; clothing and shelter were procured from this diverse and rich environment. The Hän traded with neighboring First Nations people and maintained interrelations through family connections and frequent gatherings.

Chapter 12
Dog Sleds and Danger

Lazarus' spent his first few weeks of on-the-job -training learning to work with his new dog sled team and by memorizing the routes, he would travel to deliver the mail and newspapers. He would be traveling over huge swaths of extremely rugged terrain with potential danger around every curve in the trails.

The period was the beginning of the summer months so he could make out some of the more used tracks but it was a tough learning curve, to say the least.

Frenchie and several of the mail carriers that had been doing this for a while had developed some rough maps of the areas and who should be where.

In their search for their fortunes, the prospectors moved around quite a bit, so it was a constantly changing landscape to follow.

The other mail carriers were glad that they were receiving some new help as several wanted to head back to their hometowns and countries. A person could only take this way of life for a short period.

Dog Sledding:
The Alaskan natives had been using dogs for transportation for many hundreds of years before any Russian or American pioneers ever came on the scene.

Before contact with the Russians in 1732, the *Inupiaq and Yup'ik people of the Bering Straits had already attached ski-like runners to the bottom of their kayaks so that they could glide across their frozen homeland.

In the earliest days of dog sledding the dogs were more like mixed breeds (mutts) that all had certain things in common.

The Indian Tribes were looking for dogs with an instinctive desire to pull long and hard through the toughest conditions. They had to be dogs that wanted to see what was around that next bend. They always wanted to be on the go.

Assembling a sled dog team involved picking leader dogs, point dogs, swing dogs, and wheel dogs. The lead dog is crucial, so *mushers take particular care in their training. Important as well is having powerful wheel dogs to pull the sled out from the snow. Point dogs are always behind the lead dogs. Next are the swing dogs between the point and wheel dogs. Team dogs are all other dogs in between the wheel and swing dogs. They select the dogs for their endurance, strength and speed as part of the team.

In dog sledding, Siberian Huskies or Alaskan Malamutes are the main types of dogs chosen because of their willingness to work.

Careful breeding over so many years had produced dogs with telltale physiques, which were not necessarily large dogs. For one thing, the best sled-pulling dogs have quick, efficient gaits and remarkable strength for their size. You rarely see a really good sled dog over about 55 pounds.

Getting dog teams to pull together took months of training. Frenchie and his people had trained a great team for Lazarus.

Frenchie had guessed that due to their tails and center of gravity Lizards would make excellent Mushers. He was excited when this proved to be true. Lazarus was such a natural that Frenchie reached out immediately to hire several more Lizards to work with him.

Laz loved the freedom of gliding across the ice and snow and spent all his waking hours working with his team.

After dozens of trials, with an experienced Musher that knew the trails and the prospectors, Lazarus felt confident enough to take over his duties as the first of several *Northern Lights Lizards to follow. That is the name he gave his future crew as it began to build.

Lazarus had an excellent memory. Over the next few months, he had mastered all the trails that led to the thousands of claims peppered throughout the region.

Before his mail runs the prospectors had nothing to read other than the labels on their canned goods. Many of them were so starved for something to read that they memorized the labels forward and backward.

The excitement that his arrivals produced every time he showed up at a gold claim was extremely rewarding. Each time the prospectors heard Laz's sled dogs barking they dropped their tools and came running. They knew his sled was full of mail and newspapers plus Laz had become the original Information Superhighway at least as far as 1890's Dawson was concerned.

The news was a two-way street. Each day Lazarus would head out with his sled full of newspapers, mail, and packages. He would return with outgoing mail plus his head full of all the scuttlebutt. He knew who was doing what, where, and when, amongst the thousands of prospectors.

The townsfolk couldn't wait to hear all the incoming gossip that he picked up along the way. The prospectors were a wild bunch, and they were so widespread that the Mounties couldn't hope to keep things peaceful in town and out there as well. There was always something going on, and Lazarus heard all sides. He was the one true ambassador to the area. No one would mess with their only news source. Many times he was able to defuse the mini wars. Everyone loved him.

Even though he carried some gold back from the claims, it was never enough for anyone to jeopardize their life by messing with him. Everyone knew they would be torn limb from limb if they did.

Lazarus in the News:

Laz became one of the big news stories circulating as well thanks to Bart and Jack's writing in the local papers. They had spilled the beans on Lazarus' now famous Train Robbery Escapades. The more the story was told, the wilder it became. The kids could just picture him running after the robbers with a wild look in his eyes flipping and spinning with his Ninja moves! Needless to say, it didn't take Lazarus long to become somewhat of a local celebrity.

Bart and Jack constantly picked his brain for any and all tidbits that Laz came across in his wide-ranging mail duties.

They weren't the only ones to take advantage of his growing information flow. Officer Steele and the Mounties made him an important link in keeping track of the good, bad, and ugly goings on out in the gold fields. He became so important to them that they made him an Honorary Mountie.

Lazarus was very proud of the changes in his life. Less than two years ago he was almost sent to jail, and now he was an Honorary Sheriff and Mountie to boot.

His life was changing in some other ways as well. He was building a reputation for delivering the mail even in bad weather. There was so much work to be done that he seemed to work 24/7. The new recruits to the Northern Lights Lizards had not yet arrived, so Laz had to work extremely hard. The prospectors were so happy with his dedication that they always had some extra gold dust or nuggets to slip him.

For the first time in his life, he had a bank account, and it was growing quickly. There were many other interesting changes still ahead in our young Lizard's life.

Chapter 12 Endnotes:

- Mushers: France was the first European power established in the Canadian Shield; accordingly, the couriers des Bois and the voyageurs of New France used the French word "*Marche!*", meaning "go" or "run," to command the team to commence pulling. "*Marche!*" became "*Mush!*" for English

Canadians. "Mush!" is rarely used in modern parlance, however; "Hike!" is more common in English.

- **The Northern Lights:** People at high northern latitudes sometimes experience an ethereal display of colored lights shimmering across the night sky – the aurora borealis or northern lights. What causes them?

    Those who live at or visit high latitudes might at times experience colored lights shimmering across the night sky. Some Inuit believed that the spirits of their ancestors could be seen dancing in the flickering aurora. In Norse mythology, the Aurora was a fire bridge to the sky built by the gods. This ethereal display – the aurora borealis *or* aurora australis, the northern or southern lights – is beautiful. What causes these lights to appear?

    Our sun is 93 million miles away. But its effects extend far beyond its visible surface. Great storms on the sun send gusts of charged solar particles hurtling across space. If Earth is in the path of the particle stream, our planet's magnetic field and atmosphere react.

    When the charged particles, from the sun, strike atoms and molecules in Earth's atmosphere, they excite those atoms, causing them to light up. What does it mean to excite an atom? Atoms consist of a central nucleus and a surrounding cloud of electrons encircling the nucleus in an orbit. When charged particles from the sun strike atoms in Earth's atmosphere, electrons move to higher-energy orbits, further away from the nucleus. Then when an electron moves back to a lower-energy orbit, it releases a particle of light or photon.

What happens in an Aurora is similar to what happens in the neon lights we see on many business signs. Electricity is used to excite the atoms in the neon gas within the glass tubes of a neon sign. That's why these signs give off their brilliant colors. The Aurora works on the same principle – but at a far more vast scale.

Chapter 13
River Bottom Brotherhood

Even with the incredible amount of work Lazarus was faced with he still made time to keep up with his friends. He looked forward to the Friday night meetings of the River Bottom Brotherhood.

They all had so many stories and adventures to pass around that they would talk all night practically.

Alexander was having the time of his life putting on plays and Vaudeville type Extravaganzas. He had met all the local actors, singers, musicians, dancers, and performers. He started putting on small performances at the restaurants he worked in.

He was excited about the local performer and business woman Klondike Kate. She greased the wheels and made it easy for Alexander to convince all the entertainers to join his productions. The two were dating and making plans to open a local theater of their own. There was so little to do in the town, besides hard work, that the local miners and townsfolk would search high and low for any form of entertainment.

The prospectors were widespread whereas the miners were more localized to the town.

This was wide open spaces for a man of Alexander's genius. He rapidly built a reputation for honesty and integrity in all his business dealings.

This reputation carried on throughout his life as he built his world renowned Pantages Theaters all over Canada and the United States.

The miners filled his pockets with gold for anything that would make them laugh, cry, sing or dance.

He would do anything to entertain his customers, including bringing to the stage ***Alice Teddy - The World's Only Roller Skating Bear.** Even Lazarus, with his bear phobia, got a huge laugh out of that one.

COMPLIMENTS OF

P
A
N
T
A
G
E
S

T
H
E
A
T
R
E

ALICE TEDDY
The Only Roller Skating Bear in the World.   Alice is
Five years Old and Weighs 236 Pounds.
PANTAGES THEATRE
PIONEER PRINTING CO., SEATTLE

Alex loved producing Variety and Vaudeville Shows. He and Kate became extraordinarily successful in Dawson.

Jack London worked hard at his writing and anything else that he could do to make a living. He was only 21 years old at the time so the group tried to help him anyway that they could. They worried about him.

Dawson was a tough place for most people to survive in. Jack was no exception. The food there was very expensive and in short supply. The young man did not eat as well as he should have.

Due to the shortage of certain foods like fresh fruit and vegetables, during the long winter months, many people came down with illnesses such as scurvy. A lack of vitamin C caused this problem. Many sailors that spent months at sea suffered the same infirmary.

Even with the Brotherhood trying to be the Motherhood for Jack he still came down with scurvy. This illness would shorten his stay in the Klondike; however his time there was well spent.

When he finally returned to California, his head was so full of adventures and exciting times that his future as a successful writer was assured.

Bart Bettus came to the Gold Country already a reasonably successful writer with a minor case of writer's block. He had a large enough bank account to not worry about starving. With his love for food and drink, he had little concern of having a vitamin deficiency. He could probably have sucked Vitamin C out of the cigars and whiskey bottles he enjoyed so much.

Dawson and the Yukon formed a giant reservoir of material for a writer. It was as if a dam broke for Bart. For starters, he was writing the ever popular Dime Novels "The Adventures of Lazarus Lézard." The first was about the train robbery entitled; "Lazarus Lizard and the Scales of Justice". Even though Laz's scales were not that pronounced Bart still got a real kick out of his wordplay.

Bart desperately wanted to travel to the claims with Laz but due to his size and the huge amount of mail bags and packages, there was just no way. He did follow him to a few locations on horseback. He grilled Laz nonstop for every nugget of news he could pull from him.

Once the Telegraph system connected Dawson with Vancouver in 1901, it opened the world to the adventure stories happening there. Bart had an unlimited flow of ideas and stories to send out to the eyes and minds of another generation of readers.

Part-time Members of the RBB:

There were some other local people that would sit in on some of the River Bottom Brotherhood's dinner meetings.

The Head of the Yukon Mounties Sam Steele along with some of his other Officers would drop by to keep abreast of the unique information flow that the RBB was able to unearth.

The future "Major General **"Sir"** Samuel Benfield Steele had an amazing life and story of his own.

In 1877, he was assigned to meet with Chief Sitting Bull, who, having defeated General Custer at Little Bighorn had moved with his people to Canada to escape American vengeance. Steele along with U.S. Army General Alfred Howe Terry attempted unsuccessfully to persuade Sitting Bull to return to the United States. (Most of the Sioux did return a few years later.)

During the North-West Rebellion Steele was dispatched with a small force. Missing the Battle of Batoche the Mounties were sent to move against the last rebel force led by Chief Big Bear. He was present at the Battle of Frenchman's Butte, where Big Bear's warriors defeated the Canadian forces under General Thomas Bland Strange. Two weeks later, Steele and his two dozen Mounties defeated Big Bear's force at Loon Lake, District of Saskatchewan, in the last battle ever fought on Canadian territory. The contributions of the NWMP in putting down the rebellion went largely ignored and unrewarded, to Steele's great annoyance.

By 1885, Steele held the rank of superintendent. He established an NWMP station in the town of Galbraith's Ferry, which was later, renamed Fort Steele in British Columbia after Steele solved a murder in the town. He then moved on to Fort Macleod, District of Alberta, in 1888.

Samuel gained a tremendous respect for the Native Americans. His understanding and knowledge went a long way toward his fair dealings with the Yukon Indians who weren't treated well by the gold-hungry white races that invaded their tribal lands.

If it hadn't been for men like Samuel Steele, it could have been much worse.

Officer Steele and his force made the Klondike Gold Rush one of the most orderly of its kind in history and made the North West Mounted Police famous around the world.

Aside from some Alexander's entertainment friends who periodically stopped by their meetings, there was a great man of the cloth who liked to think of himself as an Honorary Member of the RBB.

*Father William Judge was a Jesuit priest who established St. Mary's Hospital, a facility in Dawson City, which provided shelter, food and any available medicine to the many hard-luck gold miners who filled the town.

He was known as "The Saint of Dawson." He earned that name. Not only did he help save Jack London's life but also many others who became ill during the horrible long winters in Dawson.

He tried so hard to help others that he worked himself into an early grave.

Father Judge died on January 16, 1899, of pneumonia. A man of poor health to begin with, he was worn out by his exertions. The whole town mourned and turned out for his funeral. He was only 49 years of age.

The Yukon was an extremely cold and unforgiving land where a person was lucky to make it to 49, especially in those early days of the forbidding North Country.

Chapter 13 Endnotes:

- Father William Judge:

Father William Judge (April 28, 1850 – January 16, 1899) was a Jesuit priest who, during the 1897 Klondike Gold Rush, established St. Mary's Hospital. This facility in Dawson City, which provided shelter, food, and any available medicine to the many hard-luck gold miners who filled the town and its environs. For his selfless and tireless work, Judge became known as "The Saint of Dawson."

Chapter 14
Northern Lights Lizards

The other mail carriers had finished their contracts and headed back home. Lazarus was bone-weary and about at the end of his rope. The overload of work that he had single-handedly taken on was overwhelming him. Everyone teased him that he was working his tail off.

His dogs were as tired as he was. One day as he pulled back into town he had one thing on his mind, sleep!!!

His eyes were so tired that he could barely see straight. As he opened the door and stepped into Frenchie's office, he saw something that made him do a double-take. After rubbing his eyes and shaking his head to clear the cobwebs, he looked again. Sitting there before him were three strong young Lizards staring at him with hero worship in their eyes.

One of them stammered; "Oh my gosh it's him! It's **Lazarus Lézard!"** Apparently they had been reading Bart's Dime Novels.

The three jumped to their feet and started bombarding him with questions, patting him on the back and trying to pump his clawed hand.

Finally, Laz yelled **"Stop! Hold it a second!"** Even though he was glad to see several of his own kind he was just too exhausted for such nonsense.

He ordered them to Attention! He lined them up so that he could have some breathing room. He looked to Frenchie for a little help. Frenchie said; "Laz gets something to eat and hit the sack. I will get them settled in, and they can start their basic training tomorrow morning. Don't worry about your dogs. I'll take these guys out, and they can help me feed your team, and I'll introduce them to their dogs as well." Their dog teams had been put together and trained over the past few months.

Day One of the Northern Lights Lizards:

The following morning started early. Another bunkhouse had been built in anticipation of the new recruits. Lazarus had his own private room in it.

Rousting them out of their warm bunks and into the cold air of the North was a rude awakening, to say the least.

The rugged trip to Dawson had toughened them up, but the temperature of the far north is something you force yourself to handle. They were lucky that this was still partially Summer. There was enough time left of the milder weather to get them broken in.

Now that Lazarus was wide awake enough to see straight he took his first real look at the new recruits. He was pleased to see that they stood straight and could look him directly in the eye.

They still were in awe of Laz, but he could see that they each had a toughness of their own.

It would take a lot of inner strength to do the job that Laz and Frenchie were going to train them to do.

The strongest looking of the trio, whose name was Lonnie, hailed from Kansas. He actually had delivered mail there by horse-drawn wagon for several years. After hearing about Lazarus in the local paper and Dime Novels, he immediately knew this was what he wanted to do.

Lyle and Larry were two egg brothers from Detroit, Michigan. They were tough and used to cold winters. Like Lazarus, they were getting into some trouble with the law and jumped at the chance to head north.

In Detroit, they would have been forced to work in smoke-belching factories. The idea of working outdoors in fresh air appealed to them. Of course getting out of their warm bunks that morning gave them visions of the warm oily air of the factory.

The two brothers reminded Laz of himself and his egg brother Lorenzo who was having adventures of his own in Paris.

Frenchie took over the first phase of their training with mushing lessons. Working with the dog teams and the sleds would take up the first month.

During that month, Laz would take one at a time with him on his mail routes. In this way, they could familiarize themselves with the trails and meet some of their future customers. Following Lazarus' dog team with their own was great training for them.

This was really fun and exciting for the recruits. All the excitement that their arrivals caused at the camps was thrilling to the recruits. The warmth of their reception went a long way to removing the chill in their bones that the freezing trail caused.

The sourdough gold miners razzed the recruits nonstop. Laz was held in such high esteem that they looked at the new guys with skeptical eyes. They walked around them making the boys flex their biceps and semi kiddingly quizzed them mercilessly. The mail and supplies that Laz brought the miners and prospectors were one of the most important aspects of their hardscrabble lives.

Laz leaned back and let this go on because he wanted the recruits to know just how important their new jobs were to these men and the few extremely tough women who worked side by side with them.

Revolving Routes:

Weeks rolled into months, and the Northern Lights Lizards developed into a cohesive team that Lazarus became very proud to be leading.

Laz knew all the many routes. They were broken up into chunks that could be one-day mail routes.

Laz had temporarily been the sole mail carrier. This situation meant that some of the miners only received mail every three weeks.

Now with his new teams, the miners received mail once per week.

Laz knew all the routes, so he rotated with the teams one day per week. This policy gave the guys a day off each week as he took over their routes for a day. Laz could then spend days with important longer runs for medical supplies and special emergency situations.

He came to care for all three, but he felt a special bond begin to grow between Lonnie and himself.

Could that bond be, in part, the photos of Lonnie's sister Loraine that Laz couldn't take his eyes off of? She had become his long-range pen pal, and he found he could not stand the long waits for her next letter. The mail came in batches so instead of one letter, he would receive six or seven in one delivery.

He would read them so many times that he would practically suck the ink right off the pages with his eyes. Lonnie would almost gag with all the questions that Laz had. He would pepper him with questions at all times of day or night.

Lazarus' lovelorn thoughts were heating up to such a degree that he was melting the ice and snow all around him.

"Laz in Love" was the topic of the whole town. Of course, Frenchie being an utterly romantic Frenchman would wax lyrical for hours about this with anyone that would listen.

Judging by the amount of return mail Lazarus was receiving from Kansas this was not a one-sided affair. Loraine loved his letters. Lazarus was becoming a legend. His reputation had reached mythological proportions due to the wild adventure writing by his best friend, Bartholomew "Bart" Bettus.

Laz did not understand what the hubbub was all about. It was highly embarrassing to him, and he asked Bart to knock it off.

"Now don't go getting all hot under the collar Mr. Lézard. It is turning your beautiful green face all red and blotchy, by golly! Besides Laz, this has gotten bigger than the both of us. We owe it to your public!"

"What the heck do you mean '**My Public**'? No Bart, what I think you mean is that we owe it to your bank account!"

"You know Laz; sometimes it is hard to argue with your logic. Money keeps food in our stomachs and what is wrong with a good cigar or two?"

"**I don't smoke!!!**" Lazarus exclaimed loudly!

"You should try it Laz. It is quite calming for your frayed nerves!" Bart smiled as if the matter was settled. "Besides your Lady Lizard seems to like the Dime Novels I am writing."

This issue was neither the first nor the last of this ongoing topic between the two good friends.

Chapter 15
Deadly Weather

November in the Klondike can be a dark foreboding time of year. The ground was frozen to almost ten ft. deep. Today the Klondike and Yukon Rivers were frozen solid.

Winter was setting in with a vengeance. The weather could change in a hurry from bad to extremely bad.

Not much, if any, mail got through to Dawson City during these winter months. At times, there wasn't much for the Northern Lights Lizards to do other than delivering local newspapers and supplies to the extremely hardcore sour dough's that continued to work their claims in the cold dark months.

To do this in these extreme conditions, the miners had to use all types of wild equipment concoctions. They used things such as boilers to heat the frozen ground so that they could get a shovel inches into the icy bedrock.

Lazarus and the rest of the Northern Lights Lizards thought these people were crazy, but the sourdoughs were willing to pay plenty of gold to get even a local newspaper through to them. They would have paid bags of gold dust just to have the guys show up with juicy town gossip. The guys could have made the gossip up. The miners were just that starved for anything to break up the long lonely 19 hours of darkness they lived with during these winter months. The sun only popped out for about 5 hours a day. It was more like a lessening in the pitch black than actual daylight.

Delivering anything this time of year was tricky, and gambling on the weather could be a deadly game of Russian roulette. Lazarus insisted on two teams per trip. This was not a time to travel without backup.

The weather over the past few days was beginning to look extremely bleak. The town began to worry about some miners that lived out on the far fringes of the known area.

Roundups and Rescues:

It was obvious that a monster storm was developing. Over the next few days, the weather continued to deteriorate. Lazarus and Officer Steele of the Mounties had several meetings. Because Laz's NLL's knew the trails better than anyone in the Yukon, they were important to the growing situation. Each Lizard dog sled team would guide several Mounties out to the claims to check on the condition of the miners. If the weather continued to get worse, they would help bring as many as possible into town.

The four dogsled teams were loaded with as much in the way of provisions and emergency equipment as was possible.

After Laz had seen the other three teams and Mounties off, he joined his friend Sergeant Keith Harriman and made ready to head out. He didn't need more men because the two were mainly heading out to one location.

A hardheaded husband and wife team were working a claim far out past everyone else.

Everyone had tried time and time again to convince them of the danger of what they were doing.

No one had seen them in months, and there had been rumors from some of the local Indians that the woman may be pregnant. This potential situation really worried Lazarus, and he was determined to break through the bad weather to check on them.

As Officer Keith and Laz headed out, they were warned to please be careful. The Old Timers knew this was going to be an extremely dangerous storm. You could smell it in the air. The lightning strikes were everywhere. The ionization and ozone caused by the lightning gave off almost a metallic smell and taste to the air. You could see your shadow on the ground when they lite up the sky.

They were only about five miles out of town when a huge fireball of lightning struck an old dead tree next to the trail. Tree limbs and branches flew through the air like shrapnel. The force of the strike and the horrendous sound it made shook the ground so violently that Officer Harriman's horse jumped four feet off the ground trying to get out of the way as the top half of the tree ignited and hit all around them. Smoldering chunks of wood peppered the area.

Both the officer and the horse crashed to the ground. Lazarus jumped off the back of his sled and ran to them. It didn't look good. It seemed that the Mountie had dislocated his shoulder but even worse his horse was badly hurt.

Laz knew that if he followed the officer back to town he wouldn't be able to get back out again. He had a gut feeling that the couple out on their claim was in real trouble. He and Officer Harriman talked it over, and Laz elected to push on. His dog team was extremely strong and experienced. If anyone could get through it was Lazarus and his team that could do it.

Officer Harriman and his horse could make it, if somewhat painfully, back to town on their own.

Every hour of travel for Laz and his team became progressively worse. The storm was now in full gale force very much like you only experience out at sea. This was turning into a frightening blizzard. The snow and ice were blowing into his face so hard that Laz was soon completely disoriented. All he could do was continue on and pray that they were heading in the right direction. The many hours of darkness only made the situation that much worse.

For one of the first times in his life, Lazarus felt the real gut wrenching fear. He was not only worried for himself and his team; he also felt that the couple he was trying to help was in serious trouble.

He hoped that his friend Sergeant Keith and his horse were okay. The worse things got, the more his resolve crumbled. He thought he should have returned to town himself. This wicked weather was beyond anything he had ever experienced in his life.

On they pushed. Hour after hour they searched. He and his team crisscrossed the rugged terrain putting an extreme hardship on them. Hope was fading that they would find the right trail and reach the couple's cabin in the woods.

Laz lost all track of time and space. It was hard to tell left from right and even up from down. The snow and wind were swirling and seemed to be coming at them from every direction at once.

At times, he was being dragged through the snow by his team.

Finally with a small break in the constant wind and snow Lazarus saw what looked like something man made. He thought he saw a cabin in the distance. He called out to the dogs and headed in that direction. They didn't need any added encouragement from him. They were tired and sensed the cabin might bring them some rest from the storm.

It was the cabin alright but what scared Laz was the first close up view of the entrance. The door was ajar with snow build up and the wind blowing through the opening. He could see that part of the roof had collapsed into the cabin. This wreckage didn't look good at all. Lazarus was dreading going into what he knew was bad news.

He brought the team to a halt and pulled out a shovel from the emergency tools he had brought. After digging his way in he was greeted by a sight that confirmed his worst fears.

The husband and wife obviously dead and were covered with snow and debris from the caved in roof. Laz could see that they had been laying there for several days. There was nothing he could do for them.

About all he could do was bring a crew back out when the weather got better. They would retrieve the bodies for burial in the town cemetery.

This was incredibly sad for Lazarus. He hadn't really known these people as they were so far out on the fringe that the mail wasn't even delivered to them. Still life was precious to him.

The blizzard started gathering strength for what looked like another heavy assault. After covering the bodies, he brought the dogs inside and worked to seal up the doorway.

After resting the team overnight, he was ready to head back toward town. They couldn't stay there to wait out the storm due to the condition of the cabin. He was just ready to yell *"Mush"* when he thought he heard something. The dogs started yapping and looking toward the cabin. "Did you hear that boys"? Laz said to the dogs. They began barking and trying to move back toward the cabin door. "Wait there it is again. It's coming from inside the cabin!"

He went back in and started digging around through the snow and damage looking for what had caused that strange sound. He began opening cabinets and anywhere else he may have missed when he had first checked the cabin.

He pulled out a final large drawer and received the shock of his life. There under furs and swaddling blankets was small twin babies all wrapped up in an attempt to save them from the storm.

Laz was flabbergasted. Once the light hit the babies eyes, they both cried out. The fact that they could be here and are alive really shocked Laz to the bone. What should he do? He had no experience with babies'- lizard, human, or otherwise.

He looked out toward the sled and said; "What do we do now boys?" He knew this changed everything.

The babies must be starving. The mother must have been breastfeeding them so they could not have had any milk for days.

Thank God the town had heard the woman might have been pregnant. The town's women had pushed Lazarus to bring bottles, canned milk, and diapers. He had hated taking up important room in the sled for something they weren't sure of, but now it could be a lifesaver. If they got back to town, he would be forever grateful to them.

With his supplies, he was able to build a small fire and after all the struggles that only a bachelor Lizard could go through he got them changed and fed.

"What in the heck are we going to do now boys?" He exclaimed to the dogs. In this, they were no help what so ever.

The storm could last for days, and they couldn't stay where they were. The rest of the roof could fall in at any time.

The break in the storm couldn't last much longer either. He could tell it was getting ready to hit them again.

He bundled up the babies to the best of his ability and knelt next to them to pray for their dead parents and for the twin's safety. They headed back out. It was tough going right from the start. Laz knew it wasn't going to get better, and it didn't.

The blizzard rushed back in on them with brutal force. Things were not good and getting worse. The dogs were extremely brave, and they continued to push through the torture that was hitting them full in the face.

Hoping to feed and change the babies along the way was out of the question. All he could do was push on and pray for all of them but especially the little ones. "Lord they have lost their parents. They need a chance to grow up. They're just babies. If you help them, I promise I will devote the rest of my life to helping people everywhere!"

They pushed on. He could not tell if they were even going in the right direction. There was only dark and storm. With no stars to guide him, he could be going north, south, east or west.

He and the dogs were getting tired beyond anything Laz had ever imagined. He tied himself to the back of the sled. If he fell off, he would not find the sled again as the dogs pushed on. The babies would die for sure!

They were moving slower and slower. The dogs could barely take another step. All Lazarus had left was his prayers, and he was afraid that they were not going to be enough to save them. If they stopped to rest now, he knew they would not be able to start again. They would all freeze.

He was so tired that his mind began playing tricks on him. Through the storm, he imagined he saw a fire off in the distance. He could not see very far because of the white out conditions so he knew he was losing his mind.

"But what is that?" He mumbled to himself. The dogs barked. "Boys, are you losing your minds too?" He yelled out through the wind.

They began to bark more. Lazarus was almost screaming; "There! Do you see that? What in God's name is that? Have we found the gateway to Hell itself?"

Donald G. Parent

Chapter 16
Dark and Desperate Times

Lazarus had been gone now for over a week. Lonnie took over the leadership of the Northern Lights Lizards. He kept them busy so that they didn't dwell on Laz and the bad weather they were still experiencing.

The River Bottom Brotherhood began again to have their Friday meetings. Lazarus' regular chair was left untouched, and they always ordered his favorite meal set up there.

Lonnie became a new member to, "temporarily" as he said, take Lazarus' place. Bart refused to write about the possibility of his death. He knew in his heart that he would see his friend again. Hopefully, it would be in this life and not the next.

Alexander Pantages was busy putting on shows and

purchasing his first theater in the area. He and Klondike Kate were partners in the new entertainment venue. The townspeople poured in, especially during the long dark days and nights of winter. Cabin fever contributed largely to their bottom line. Bags of gold were flowing in for the two lovebirds.

So much gold passed through the towns businesses that there was money to be made by anyone who dared to crawl on the frozen ground under the floorboards of the raised buildings to scoop up what spilled down through the cracks from above.

It drove Bart crazy that his belly was too big to get under the floorboards. Of course, he said this jokingly as he would never have messed up one of his fancy suits by crawling around in the frozen ice and mud like that.

The Mounties were kept busy this time of year with all the dust-ups caused by raw nerves that built up with so many hours of darkness. The lack of sunlight caused tempers to flair. There was an upswing in everything from wife beatings to suicides. People craved sunlight and the lack of vitamin D that they received from the sun contributed to other health problems like scurvy that was also indirectly caused by the dark. In the winter, there was no fresh fruit to be had.

Jack London was having trouble due to this. Scurvy was causing his face to break out in ugly sores, and he even had trouble walking due to pain in his legs.

Father William Judge did everything he could for Jack but come the summer he would advise Jack to head back to California where there was plenty of sunlight and fresh fruit.

The whole town was counting the months until the days grew longer and happiness would return to their lives.

The only people that didn't seem to be bothered by the winter were the *Tr'ondek Hwech'in native people of the area. They would come and go with their dog teams in just about any weather conditions.

Their ancestors had been living in the Klondike for thousands of years, and this was home to them.

No one had seen Chief Isaac for some time, but that was normal. The Indians didn't worry about him. He was like the sun. It would show up eventually.

Chapter 17
Fire and Ice

"Boys I am sure I see *Fire* up ahead!" Lazarus cried out again to the dogs. "I am losing it aren't I?" He was cold and tired, but his fear and imagination were giving him a spike of adrenaline. 'This must be like a mirage to a thirsty man,' he thought to himself.

The sled dog team had been dragging him behind them for miles, but now he stood up straighter and gripped the handles with renewed strength. If he hadn't tied himself to the sled, he would have been left miles back frozen in the team's tracks.

"There it is again. I know I am seeing things boys, but I could swear that there is a huge bonfire up ahead! I know that cannot be. What is that big shape moving around it? Let's move boys. These two babies need us to go on."

The dogs were getting agitated and beginning to bark and move faster toward Laz's phantom vision. He thought they were going crazy too. "Was this what they called mass hysteria?" he mumbled.

All of a sudden the team broke through the storm and frozen ground into a cleared area with a huge fire at its center.

All the snow and ice was melted away, and the trees around the perimeter had been singed. What Lazarus saw was so far from reality that he knew he must be in the Afterlife. He again thought he was at the gates of hell. He knew he had succumbed to the storm and passed through the veil between life and death itself.

Lazarus's mind whirled back to Chief Wovoka in Wyoming and his stories of Giant Dragons flying through the skies. Lazarus had thought that the Chief's wild ramblings were just the dreams of an old Indian Shaman.

How could he now be staring at a huge Dragon standing behind the fire if he weren't in the next life? There was no such thing as dragons.

With a sound that vibrated through the ground and up Laz's legs and into his head the Dragon spoke! **"Ahhh Lazarus, there you are! I have been looking for you!"**

Lazarus cried out, "What are you? Who are you? Is this Hell? I feel the heat. What did I do to end up down here?"

The Dragon's burst of laughter felt like a huge earthquake. What was next a crack in the earth to swallow him up? **"No, No"** the dragon laughed, **"This is not hell although this storm is another form of it all its own!"**

"Who am I you ask? You may call me Lantern. You could not pronounce my actual name without a lot of practice."

"I am not dead?" Lazarus sputtered.

"No, you are not although we were worried. By the look of you, it was close."

"Oh my God the babies! The babies need help! I must check on the babies!!!" Lazarus yelled out.

"We had high hopes that you would find them and bring them to us!"

Lazarus dug into the sled and felt around. He was extremely relieved when he felt movement. "I have milk." He mumbled. "We must heat it up and help them!" He was babbling from the shock of the last few minutes. He still wasn't sure if all this was real or if he had actually lost his mind. With a wary eye toward the fictional creature, he pulled the babies out into the light and heat radiating from the fire.

The fear for the babies made him forget that he was talking to an impossible creature in the middle of a blizzard, in the middle of a clearing, and in the middle of nowhere!!!

"Yes, we will feed and change their clothing. Step back and I will start a smaller fire to heat their milk and dry yours and their clothing and blankets."

Lazarus almost passed out from shock when Lantern opened his huge mouth and with a tiny puff started a small pile of wood on fire.

"Now that was nothing, Lazarus," Lantern said when he saw the shocked look on his face. "You should have been here when I cleared this area and started the bonfire!" Lantern said with another booming laugh. "Once the twins are comfortable I will take you to a safe place."

"Where is that?" Laz asked with a nervous look in his eye.

"All in good time Lazarus, all in good time!" He said with a wink and a smile.

Chapter 18
Flights of Fancy

Lazarus was sleepwalking from fatigue and the shocks the last hour had brought him. He was beyond surprised or anything at this point.

Lantern had known about Lazarus from stories brought to him by the Native Indian Pipeline. He had prepared to go out and help him. Even as strong as he was he could only search so far in a raging storm like the one they had dealt with.

He also knew about the possibility of the babies and was prepared for this challenge as well.

He had been putting out a psychic beacon to the sled dog team, and it had finally worked.

The Dragon asked Lazarus to feed his team from the supplies he had flown in. Lazarus noticed a pile of food and water. This went a long way to erasing some of his shock and fears.

After they had been well fed, Lantern placed his huge head next to the dogs for a second. The team cocked their heads as if they heard something. They then curled up next to the fire and went right to sleep.

Lazarus said; "How did you do that?" He had noticed in some of their communications that Lantern's mouth had not moved. Another mystery to go with everything else his mind was spinning from.

"Don't worry about your team Lazarus. I have told them that I will return to them soon. They need to rest and regain their strength"!

Laz was so brain dead at this point that it didn't even surprise him to see the small carriage that was strapped to

Lanterns back. The Dragon spread one of his huge wings to the ground and told Laz to pick up the babies and climb aboard.

Lazarus said out loud shaking his head; "What could be more natural. I'm going to climb up the wing of a giant mythical talking creature that shoots fire out of its face!!! It says it is taking us somewhere safe. It couldn't possibly be any worse than this storm? Let's find out!" He hugged the babies to his chest and climbed aboard.

He was surprised at how warm and comfortable the carriage was inside. It must have been being heated by Lanterns internal flame. Laz let out a huge whoop when they lifted up into the air. The dogs stirred back on the ground for a second and then went back to sleep. The babies were full and warm. They seemed content.

Lazarus could see the storm swirling around the outside of the carriage. The babies went right to sleep. Laz was also warm and comfortable for what seemed like the first time in months. He soon fell into a deep sleep himself.

Cambria:
Lazarus yawned and slowly opened his eyes. They were flying over frozen peaks with howling winds blasting snow and ice up and over their tips.

All of a sudden a sight opened up right before his eyes that made him think that he must still be dreaming.

The sun was shining down through a huge circle in the clouds that must have been a hundred miles across.

In the Eye of the Storm:
He could see a large valley surrounded by the high peaked mountains they had been flying over.

Behind them, Laz could see the mountain peaks being blasted by the storm.

In front and below he could see what he thought were rolling green hills, lakes, and farmlands.

He thought, 'Where on earth are we? Is this still the Earth?'

Rumbling up from deep beneath the carriage and into his head he heard;

"Welcome to Cambria Lazarus."

Cambria Township

"What is this place" Lazarus blurted out loud. **"Quiet Lazarus, you'll wake up the babies! You can speak to me over short distances by just thinking what you would like to say!"**

Lazarus thought 'What the heck is next? Crickets shooting out of your nose!' Lantern thought this was the funniest thing he had ever heard. He laughed so hard that it shook the whole carriage and woke the babies anyway. They began to squirm around, and he could tell that they were hungry again.

"To answer your question, this is my home. Cambria means "The Healing Place" and you shall see this for yourself over the next few days."

They were flying rapidly down toward what looked like a picturesque town square. There was a crowd forming. The people were waving up at them, and Laz could see they were really happy and excited. What amazed him was one face he thought was familiar. In the middle of the group he thought he could see Chief Isaac staring up at him with a huge smile on his face.

Lantern landed gently next to the crowd, and several individuals climbed up on the dragon to help Lazarus and the babies down.

Several women reached out and cooed to the babies. They took them into their arms. Laz wanted to pull them protectively back, but Lantern told him not to worry. **"Relax, Lazarus. The babies will be well cared for. They knew that they were coming and are ready for them."**

Chief Isaac grabbed Laz in a bear hug and said, "Lazarus I knew if anyone could save those babies it would be you!"

Laz' mouth was moving, but he couldn't get any words out. The Chief said, "Relax Lazarus. I know you have a million questions, and there will be enough time to get most of them answered for you.

Lantern took to the air. "Where is he going?" Laz asked.

"He is heading back to take care of your dogs until we can return you to them, said the Chief. He will move them to a safe place. Your friends in Dawson are worried sick so you won't be able to stay long this time."

"What do you mean this time?"

"The Ancient Ones will explain this all to you along with answering your other questions. They have had plans for you for some time. The storm and the babies just speeded up the progression a little."

"My people have been working with the Ancient Ones for many centuries. I consider Cambria as my home away from home."

"So this is where you disappear to all the time." Lazarus blurted out!

"Actually, Lazarus this is just part of my travels, albeit an extremely important part. My most important decisions for my people get planned out here."

"Because we know each other I have been elected to be your Cambrian guide. You will be surprised at the mix of people and animals you will find here. There are many of my people here because as I have said, we have worked with the Ancient One's since my people first came to this land.

"I have been an ambassador to Cambria since Lantern saved me from an early death, due to a run-in with an angry Polar Bear. He may seem young but as you will find out Dragons live for a very long time."

"Most of the people and animals you will see here were also saved from deadly situations and the people that are still here have elected to stay. As you can see, it is a quite pleasant place to live."

"In a way, you are the first of the Lizard race to make it here."

Laz asked, "What do you mean by 'In a way?"

"That is another subject the Ancient Ones will explain to you far better than I can."

Aside from the Inuit's (mostly from the Tr'ondek Hwech'in tribes) Lazarus saw quite some white, black and brown faces with some Asians as well.

The Chief explained that the Dragons and his Inuit people had saved Russian trappers, sailors, explorers, and others that found themselves in near death situations. Some elected to stay and even went and brought their wives back to live here with them. The ones that decided to leave were sworn to secrecy and became traveling ambassadors for peace, collecting and bringing back information to the Ancient Ones. This was a worldwide network of trusted people who owed their lives to Cambria.

Lazarus saw several Dragons flying around in the distance and asked: "Are the Dragons like Lantern the Ancient Ones?"

"Well, Laz the Dragons live for extremely long periods of time. For the last several thousand years they have declined in numbers to the point that there are only a few left. Lantern and a couple left like him are hundreds of years old, but even they are not the Ancient Ones. They are much older, and there are only three left on the planet. They all are living here for the few years that they have to remain. Dragons were numerous and a leftover from the dinosaur days on earth. Because of their huge brains and their ability to fly and use fire they outlasted the other dinosaurs that were more or less their ancestors. Any more information you will get from the Ancient Ones themselves tomorrow. Today you need to regain your energy by eating and sleeping."

Lazarus asked, "OK, but just answer me this! How could this place possibly exist here so far in the frozen north?"

"Well Lazarus I am not a scientist but what I understand is that this is a unique spot on earth. The mountains surrounding us and even the valley floor are riddled with thermal hot springs. The rising heat causes a barrier that holds back the cold. That may be a simplistic explanation but take a look around. As you can see, it is working!"

Chief Isaac introduced Laz around to the crowd in a huge meeting hall/cafeteria. Some of the great things they had in Cambria were wonderful gardens. There were fruit and vegetables everywhere. As to be expected in a land named "The Healing Place" all their meals were mostly vegetarian, but the sumptuous feast of salads, pasta, bread, and desserts was magnificent. Lazarus couldn't get enough of the hot soups after almost freezing to death.

There were plenty of chickens for eggs and cows so milk and cheese were in abundance as well.

They got more protein and fat from the large schools of salmon and other fish also available.

The Inuits that lived here did miss their caribou, moose, blubber and other meats but they did travel to visit their people in the summer months where the tribes didn't have the huge abundance of fruits and vegetables. Meat and especially the fats from walrus, seals and whales were an extremely important part of their diet.

Lazarus was led upstairs and given a room with the largest, softest, bed he had ever tucked his tail into. He curled up and slept like one of the babies who were now safe and content themselves.

Chapter 19
The Ancient Ones

Lazarus woke the next morning not only refreshed but for the first time in quite a while he woke up completely worry free! The babies were safe, and so were his dogs. Chief Isaac had told him that Officer Harriman and his horse had made it back, and so had all the search teams that his Northern Lights Lizards had guided on their rescue missions. It was totally amazing that such a bad a storm had caused so few deaths and injuries. Sending out the teams had been a real success.

The only deaths had been to the mother and father of the twins which was really sad, but it could have been so much worse.

As he would learn Chief Isaac had an amazing information collecting network. Between the Flying Dragons and the traveling abilities of his native people the Chief seemed to be abreast of all the news everywhere.

The one thing that began to bother Laz as he settled into his new surroundings was the worry that his disappearance was causing the town of Dawson and all his friends there. He was ready to head back immediately. He knew however that he couldn't leave with so many questions rolling around in his head.

Chief Isaac met him the next morning. Laz asked to see the twins. As soon as he saw them, he knew that they would be well loved and taken care of.

They then had breakfast. Laz could not believe there was food like this in this part of the world. "Chief how the heck can you go back to eating dried fish and whale blubber after a meal like this?"

Isaac just laughed, "Why do you think I disappear from Dawson so often?"

"You have the most important meeting of your life in a few hours Lazarus. The last three of the Ancient Ones wish to speak with you. Afterward, we will have a meeting with the Cambria Ambassadors that are in the valley right now."

"I know this is rushing everything, but we have to get you back to Dawson while we can still explain away your absence."

Lazarus was okay with this as he wanted to see his friends back in the Klondike. Even still the fabulous meals and that bed last night made him think; 'Wait a minute. What's the rush? Dawson is a hard place and after all Lonnie's sister, Loraine isn't there. I could get used to a place like this in a hurry.'

After breakfast, they went outside where a large dragon was waiting to take Laz to the Ancient Ones. It shocked him again to be so close to what he had thought of as a mythical creature. Like everyone else he had heard of dragons since he was a young lizard. The stories of dragons had been passed down from the earliest days of recorded history, but they had been thought of as just myths and children's tales.

To climb on the back of this magnificent creature and lift off the ground was beyond anything he could have imagined. Up they went toward the side of the mountains. A huge cave, on the side of a cliff, opened up, and they landed just inside the opening. It had stone carvings and was like a portal to another dimension.   **"Follow the cave!"** boomed in his head from his flying chauffeur. **"I will be here waiting for you when you return."**

With nerves jangling, he headed further into the cave. Just as it was getting too dark to see where he was going, he spotted a lessening in the pitch black much further down the tunnel. The sides of the cave were like glass. He could visualize the dragons blasting away the rock with their fiery breath. He truly hoped to blast this long cave had gotten any aggressive behavior out of their systems. He did not want to become a crispy critter. He trusted Chief Isaac so he kept walking.

Coming into the light was as shocking as it was breathtaking. He was now in a gigantic opening filled with beauty everywhere he looked. There were columns that appeared to be of glass reaching all the way up to the cavern roof that was filled with ambient light. There were also hundreds of glass statues and sculptures in many colors. The statues were of humans, animals, and what he took to be mythical creatures such as Unicorns, Pegasus, and other strange sights that Lazarus couldn't stop looking at.

A Voice came out of nowhere and everywhere, **"Welcome Lazarus to our humble home!"** The sound filled his head much like the huge pipe organ at his favorite cathedral back home in New York. Off in the distance, he saw movement. **"Yes please come this way. We have been looking forward to this meeting for some time. We have had many humans make it to Cambria, but you are the first of our distant cousins to make the journey this far into the North!"**

Lazarus walked into the presence of what appeared to be three extremely old creatures. They were Dragons but obviously of a very advanced age.

Surprisingly there were some couches and chairs that could not have been used by beings that large. Laz suspected that they must be for guests. **"Why yes Lazarus we do get guests. We even had a special chair made for you right here."**

This information surprised him as he hadn't said anything out loud. He still wasn't used to this way of conversing.

"The three of us have been together for several thousand years. We now speak as one. Our jaws don't work as well any longer, so if you don't mind, we will speak in what you would call telepathy. You may speak or just think your thoughts."

"What do you mean by distant cousins?" Lazarus said. He was thinking 'This will take some practice to speak with only my mind. I will have to watch what I think.'

"Don't worry! After so many years nothing you could think would surprise or upset us. We already know you well enough to have allowed you to be brought here. We were really excited when we heard that you were coming to Dawson. For a long time, we had been trying to figure out a good way to make contact with our race of cousins so to speak."

The Ancient History of War:

"Over the years, we were forced to learn telepathy for self-preservation. We are the last of what was once a great race. Your species of lizard is, in fact, an offshoot of the dragon genes that we share in common. There are hundreds of other species of lizard that don't share the genes that gave us both our intelligence.

There is much to tell you in a short period, so please make yourself comfortable."

Laz settled into his custom made a chair and was surprised to be brought tea by a Native Indian.

"Lazarus please meet *Chief Catsah. He has been our friend for many years, and we would be lost without him. We are not capable of doing much for ourselves any

longer. He even made that wonderful chair you are sitting in. You will notice he designed it to accommodate your tail."

Lazarus wondered if he had made all the fantastic statues. "No, actually we made these over the centuries. It was a hobby for us when we could still get around. The glass statues and columns were made with a type of sand that we blasted with our fire. We enjoyed that and do miss the creativity"!

Laz was going to have to get used to having all his thoughts spill out like a leaking bucket.

Catsah said, "I am very happy to meet you, Lazarus. I have heard so much about your adventures on your way to Dawson and all the good things you have done since you got there."

"It seems you all have quite a flow of information for being so far out of the loop," Laz said.

"Actually, we have built a huge news network, Lazarus. My people have been working out of Cambria for several thousand years. Our race has a wonderful working relationship with The Ancient Ones. You will be surprised at how many ambassadors we have. We have a number now from the other races of humans as well. Hopefully, you will become the first from your race of Lizards."

"So why are there so few Dragons left?" Asked Laz.

"Well, that is a long and sad story, Lazarus. It all began many thousands of years ago. The race of Dragons was here at the time of the dinosaurs long before humans walked the earth"......................

Lazarus settled in as the story unfolded. The voice in Lazarus' head rumbled on...

"The dinosaurs ruled the earth from 65 through 265 million years ago. Our ancestors were considered a type of

Pterodactyl or flying Pterosaur that existed during the Jurassic and Cretaceous periods. Dragons were an offshoot of these flying dinosaurs much in the way dragons and your type of lizard split off from each other.

Over millions of years, our brains developed and grew larger than the other dinosaurs. We had very few offspring, but we lived exceptionally long lives. This longevity allowed us to flourish and to develop a comfortable society. Due to our ability to fly we lived in cliff dwellings much like this one we are in now. We did not yet have our ability with fire, so we had to find existing caves and dig them out larger. Fortunately, our claws work much like yours only much larger. Our claws allowed us to dig, build and use tools.

We lived peaceful lives and chose to become herbivores so that we did not have to kill to eat.

We are not positive about the timeline but about 65 million years ago a giant asteroid hit the earth. This along with a huge amount of volcanic activity caused the extinction of all the dinosaurs and most of our ancestors as well. Because of our intelligence, some of us were able to survive by finding places like Cambria.

Because most of the earth became extremely cold, it caused us to develop another survival tool. We gained our ability to have an internal fire source.

Over millions of years, the environment of the world changed for the better, and the race of man came into being. They reproduced rapidly and were horribly aggressive toward us. They feared our size and fire abilities. We tried to communicate with them many times, but it did no good. They had not yet developed a strong intelligence. They were still more animal than modern man. Whenever our races came together, the Humans attacked us. They considered it a war. We did not wish this as we were not aggressive at all.

They multiplied so fast that they outnumbered us thousands to one. Their huge numbers almost led to our total extinction.

The few of us that remained understood that the only thing we could do for our survival was to disappear to Cambria. The humans believed that they had wiped us out.

This brought a form of peace for us. Because of the small area that we can feel safe in it has led to only a handful of us reproducing here.

The local native Indians are also a peace loving people and we have had a wonderful relationship with them. Unfortunately, gold has brought other humans into closer contact. We did not believe that they would ever come to such a forbidding place such as the land that surrounds our healing place. The separation of our races may no longer be the case.

"That is why we are reaching out to individuals such as you Lazarus. By sending out friends of ours all over the world as Ambassadors, we hope to stop the fear and hatred of us.."

Lazarus was horrified by what had happened to his ancestors.

"Of course, you will have my help! Tell me what it is that I can do?"

"For now continue on with what you are doing. You have already built up a great reputation in the town of Dawson. Through the writing of your friend Bartholomew Betus, you are becoming a heroic figure in the United States and Canada. You have already made important friends like the lawman Charlie Siringo, your friend from the train robbery and also Officer Samuel Steele of the Mounties.

You are exactly the individual that we need as an ambassador to the race of Lizards and humans alike."

"Chief Isaac will be your lifeline to us. Whenever you wish to get out of the cold for a bit, he can arrange to have you meet Lantern north of Dawson. He will fly you here."

"Someday once you are ready to leave Dawson we would like to supply funds and everything you will need for world travel. We want you to be an important part of our information network. We would like you to make friends by doing good deeds wherever you go."

"Sorry for reading your mind but we understand that you have someone named Lorraine that you would like to visit. Perhaps we can help with that once summer gets here." It was funny to see a green face turn red. Chief Catsaw couldn't stop laughing.

With his mind spinning about his future, he was flown back down to the village

It was almost time for Lazarus to leave Cambria as a new ambassador. Chief Isaac had arranged a meeting with several other ambassadors that happened to be in Cambria at this time.

Lazarus was surprised to see several Indians that he had talked with before in Dawson but what knocked him to his knees was Frenchie standing there with a huge smile on his face.

With a wink, Frenchie said, "Sorry, Laz, but I am sure you can understand why I couldn't say anything about Cambria and the Ancient Ones before. I can't wait for you to get back to Dawson. It has been hard holding in the secret of you still being alive! Especially from Bart who has been driving everyone crazy wanting us to keep searching for you."

"I just got here, and I will be flown back soon. I need to make a quick report to the "Three Oldies on the Hill" No one in Dawson knows that I am gone."

Lazarus didn't know how many more surprises he could take. He was happy to join Frenchie as an ambassador, and he was excited about the worldwide work the Ancient Ones had laid out for him.

The babies were being taken care of by a young couple from Canada who had made a home in Cambria. Frenchie would try to find any relatives the couple that died, may have had but that didn't look promising. No one knew anything about them or exactly where they were from. They never received mail from home, and they had been really private about their background. Many people that tried their luck as prospectors in the Yukon were actually running from their past

Chief Isaac was going back to Dawson with Lazarus. The cover story would be that he had found Lazarus and his dogs wandering near death. He had nursed them back to health with the help of an Indian family that lived and hunted in the north. The Chief actually kept his sled dog team with them whenever he was flown into Cambria. Lantern had moved Laz's dogs there as well.

After goodbyes all around the two were flown to collect their dogs and sleds. Laz's dogs were very excited to see him. Lantern wanted to hear everything. Afterward, Lantern took off back home as the weather was holding and it would now be a much easier trip back to Dawson for Laz and the Chief and their two dog teams.

Donald G. Parent

Chapter 20
Back From the Dead

As they got closer to Dawson Lazarus and the Chief, along with their teams started causing quite a ruckus. People were calling out to them and waving. They ran after them yelling, "Look, everybody, it's Lazarus. He ain't dead after all!!!! It's a miracle!"

Word spread like wildfire. People came pouring out of homes and businesses wondering what all the noise and hubbub was.

Surrounded by the townsfolk, he was suddenly yanked off his feet and spun around as if he were back in the storm. "Bart put me down! You're going to break me in half, you maniac."

"By golly you're alive, by golly" was all he could say. Everyone was patting him on the back and yelling questions faster than he could answer them. "Where have you been? What happened? Are you alright?"

"I could be alright if this gorilla would put me down!" he laughed. "Let me catch my breath and I will tell you all about my ordeal."

Laz turned his dogs over to Frenchie to be feed and taken care of. He silently got a kick out of the acting job Frenchie was doing pretending to be as shocked and surprised as the rest of the town.

He had to use his acting skills to spin the yarn that he and the Chief had put together to explain away his absence. "After I found the poor couple dead in their cabin I tried to head back to town but became hopelessly lost." Of course, there was no mention of the babies or Cambria. "Thank the

Lord that Chief Isaac found us or me and my team would have been frozen stiff to the ground by now.

The Northern Lights Lizards were extremely happy to see him. Lonnie was thrilled that he could now write his sister Lorraine with the whole story and its happy ending. No mail had been going out, so he hadn't told her that Lazarus was missing.

After all the excitement of Lazarus' return, the town slowly got back to business as usual. The weather kept improving. The frozen months passed and mail started coming in again.

Lazarus made many trips to study with the Ancient Ones. They had so much to teach him. There were many long conversations regarding his future work. They made a list of potential ambassadors. His brother Lorenzo would be an excellent choice for Europe. The Judge, who had sent him here in the first place, was already an ambassador along with some important people in the US and Canada. It appeared that the judge did know what he was doing when he sent Lazarus north. The Ancient Ones had been looking for someone exactly like him. The Judge had kept his eye on Lazarus for the right time to convince him to go north. He knew it would only be a matter of time before the young Lizard would end up in front of him in his courthouse

Arrangements were made for Lazarus to contact the Judge and many others of the ambassadors.

Love Marches North:

Lorraine had moved. She was now in Seattle to be closer to Laz and her brother Lonnie. Even though they had not met face to face their friendship was growing stronger and stronger through all the letters they wrote to each other almost daily.

Arrangements were in the air, literally, for their first meeting. The plans were being flown back and forth by Lantern, to the Ancient Ones.

The Ancient Ones asked to meet the other Northern Lights Lizards. One by one they were brought into Laz's Cambrian support team of ambassadors and flown to Cambria.

Lazarus hoped to recruit people like Marshal Charlie Siringo, Officer Steele of the Mounties and people like Sebastiano and Joseph Salerno of Little Italy in Omaha. He mustn't forget Ed Towse, the reporter for the Cheyenne Daily Sun and Wovoka the Indian Medicine Man whose magic tricks mesmerized Laz in Cheyenne, Wyoming. He had a feeling that Wovoka knew much more than just the legends already.

Some of them would take some convincing. Telling them about Dragons in the frozen North might give them pause to suspect his sanity, but he knew people like Wovoka would love this. Indian Legends are full of Dragon lore from The Thunderbird to the Legend of the Earth Dragon and much more.

Of course, there was no way to keep all this from Bart. Lazarus did speak with the Ancient Ones regarding all of these humans and his Northern Lights Lizards. Some were authors, and some were newspapermen. Convincing them of the importance of secrecy would be a tricky part of the work Lazarus had ahead of him.

The Ancient Ones knew that their time of concealment could end at any time. That was why they were reaching out to Lazarus and bringing in more ambassadors to smooth the way.

Chapter 21
Lenny and Lizzie
Join the Family Business

"Well children," Lazarus said, "Many things happened rather quickly after that. In the summer, I was able to leave Lonnie in charge of the Northern Lights Lizards and headed back up to Skagway. There I boarded a boat to Seattle to meet Lorraine. Bart came along just in case I needed a best man, and I did!"

"Loraine and I had fallen in love through our hundreds of letters, and you could say it was love at first sight when we finally looked into each other's eyes."

"She came back with me to Dawson and quickly fit right in. Bart loved her as did the rest of the town."

"We made one long trip to France which we called our belated honeymoon. We spent a month with my brother Lorenzo who jumped at the chance to become an ambassador to Cambria.

Over the years, he also made several trips to meet with the Ancient Ones."

"Later during WWI and II, through his work as a newspaper reporter, and spy, he was able to send us valuable information about conditions in Europe. As your mom and dad, I am sure to have told you he became famous as Lorenzo Lézard The "Spy with a Thousand Faces." One of these days I must tell you stories about his incredible adventures."

Your Grandma and I stayed in Dawson for a few more years until we decided it was time for some little Lizards of our own."

"We set up our home base in Seattle. Yep, your dad Laurence was our first egg hatched. Later came some brothers and sisters for him."

"My work for the Ancient Ones forced me to be gone for long periods of time but by then we had recruited some members of our race to move to Seattle to help us. This was a Godsend for your grandmother during my trips. She had good company and your father, aunts and uncles kept her quite busy. Of course, Bart visited many times as did others from Dawson on their travels back and forth to Dawson and other parts of the world."

"Every time Bart showed up there was another little Lizard or two to greet him at the door. All he could say was, **"By golly** here are more to hug! Lazarus, you will need a bigger house!!!""

"Of course, Alexander Pantages visited often. He stayed with us while building his second theater, *The Crystal, in Seattle. He and Klondike Kate had had a parting of the ways. They were both just way too headstrong and fiery to make it as a couple. That made me a little sad!"

"Our home was always busy with exciting guests like Wovoka, who our kids loved. They would make him do magic tricks for hours."

"They always looked forward to Charlie Siringo, who helped me teach them self-defense and told them stories of being a Marshal in the Wild West."

"Ed Towse from Cheyenne would stop by on his travels, and we all loved it when Sebastiano and Joseph Salerno would spend some time with us as well. Their Italian cooking would fill the house with friends and neighbors alike. You could smell their cooking for blocks."

"Sam Steele of the Mounties stayed in touch and went on to become Major General Sir Samuel Benfield Steele. He was an extremely influential human that opened many important doors for my work representing the Ancient Ones."

"Grandpa what can we do? We want to be involved," exclaimed Lizzie. "Yeah I want to help too!" Lenny said jumping up.

"Well, children I wasn't going to have you get involved until you were a little older but your father was about your age when he started working with us."

"Our father is an ambassador?" They both sang out at the same time. "We thought he just worked at his bank?"

"Why yes kids he does work at the bank that he started. His job is very important. The Ancient Ones have a fortune in things like gems, gold, and silver. This was collected over the centuries. However, it is harder to spend than paper money. Your father has done an extremely important job. By turning their wealth into bankable assets he has been able to invest for them around the world."

"His hard work has ensured enough money to be available to smooth out the rough spots that will crop up as the world learns about the Dragons past and more importantly their presence in today's world."

"He also oversees travel arrangements and funding for our many Ambassadors. The money is used to do thousands of good deeds worldwide. Someday once their presence becomes known, we hope that their many great works helping humans and Lizards alike will go a long way to stopping the backlash that once took place between the races. The Dragons are too peaceful and could not stand another conflict! "

"What do you want us to do Grandpa?"

"Well for starters you, of course, must swear never to reveal any of this to anyone without an agreement from the Council of Ambassadors. Your mother, father, and all ambassadors make this pledge and live by it! I had expected this and already have been given the go-ahead by the counsel regarding you two. Your family is extremely important members of the council, and we expected you would someday join us as well."

"Next, you will be trained by your parents and me on how to turn bad relationships into good ones. This training begins tomorrow, and you will learn how to live happily with the other children of all races at your school. That will be your initial training ground for all the future work you will be asked to do once you are full-fledged Cambrian ambassadors."

Of course, there will be training in martial arts, languages, and history so you will understand how it is important not to make the same mistakes that happened in the distant past!"

Lenny and Lizzie looked to their Grandfather with wonder in their eyes. Their whole future was taking a complete turn toward greatness and adventure that they were just beginning to comprehend.

They were ready and willing to return to their school to begin their future in earnest!

The End!

Or is it?

Watch for future Adventures with Lennie, Lizzy, and Lazarus; and simply turn the page for a look at Lorenzo Lézard, "The Spy with a Thousand Faces"!!!

Here's a Sneak Peek from the upcoming book by:

Don Parent
Book #2 of the

Lézard Family Chronicles

Featuring Lorenzo Lézard

The Spy with 1000 Faces

In:

The Tong Wars: Trouble in Little Chinatown
And Other Adventures

Exciting Topics in Book 2 Adventures:

- **Lorenzo's Early Life:** Paris and the Mean Streets of New York
- **Early Training:** Becoming an Actor and Circus Performer, War Correspondent and Master Spy
- **Kung Fu and the Tong Wars**
- **Fighting "The Enigma"** A fearsome Shaolin Kung Fu Master
- **Attempted Murder under the Big Top**
- **Saving the Circus**

Adventure #1
The Tong Wars: Trouble in Little Chinatown

Chapter 1
The Early Years

You might wonder how it is possible that a lizard, hatched in France and growing up on the mean streets of New York, could become Europe's most Famous War Correspondent, and International Spy. Well, that is a very interesting story that now needs to be told.
We must start at the beginning.

The Early Years:
Lorenzo and his Egg brother Lazarus were hatched in Paris, France in 1872. They were the oldest of five offspring.
Their father Lawrence Lézard eked out a meager living as a chimney sweep. This occupation was not his first choice, but it was all he could find and afford the tools for if he wanted any work at all. The implements of this trade were simple and inexpensive. Few companies were hiring Lizards during this tough period of history. He had to become self-employed or starve.
These were hard times in all Europe. Many small wars were happening in the ramp up years to WWI. The competition, for any work, was tough and heartbreaking.

Abusing Children:
Many unethical individuals used orphans, and children off the streets, as Chimney Boys. In the early 1800's small boys were forced into hard labor. Their small size allowed them access to the small sometimes meandering flues that led up to the roof.

In the 1820's an engineer from Bristol, England, Mr. Joseph Glass, was widely recognized as the inventor of modern chimney cleaning equipment.

These special brushes and long cane handle allowed Lawrence to do this type of work and deal with the small spaces. His long tail gave him extra leverage to work in tight quarters and gave him excellent balance on rooftops as well.

He was lucky to find any work at all in those early times.

He was also lucky to find a business partner like Petit Pierre LeBow, who fit the bill perfectly.

Petit Pierre had been his stage name as a tiny acrobat and clown in the traveling *Cirque Medrano.

Pierre grew tired of the constant travel of circus life, so he pitched his tent with Lawrence in Paris. He thought the idea of a lizard chimney sweep was the

funniest thing he had ever heard. It made him feel as
though he was still in the circus where he had known
several lizard friends and performers. Pierre had
become friends with Lawrence, over the years, when
the circus did stops in Paris. Laurence did part time
side work for the circus when it toured near his home
so that he could get free tickets for his kids.
Pierre was one of the many midgets that toured with
circus companies.
Due to his tiny size and acrobatic skills, Pierre could
fit into the nooks and crannies that were a tough fit
for his partner Lawrence.

**The Luck of the
Sweep:**
Legend has it that
the year 1066 King
William of Britain
was saved by a
chimney sweep,
who pushed him
out of the way of a
runaway horse,
and carriage. As a
reward, the king
invited the
chimney sweep to
his daughter's
wedding. Ever since it has been considered to be good
luck to have a chimney sweep at a wedding or special
event, or even visit your house. Also, the king
declared all chimney sweeps to be lucky, and allowed

their profession only to wear top hats, which became a custom previously reserved for royalty and the gentry. It also became lucky for a sweep to wear 13 buttons on his jacket, and legend has it that a sweep can cancel out any bad luck.

Lawrence didn't get invited to any fancy weddings and just felt lucky to put enough food on the table to feed his large family.

He was well known as a very hard worker, but it was tough for everyone in Europe at that time.

Things continued to become harder for the family until one day Lawrence received a letter from relatives in New York telling him there was plenty of work if he would be willing to move his family there. This idea caused a huge dilemma as he could only scrape up enough money to move part of the family, at first. They had to leave several of their offspring with relatives if they were going to make things work. They would leave one of the two oldest brothers to help with the temporary transition.

Lorenzo was happy to stay as he had many friends, and was already involved in the theater through school. His aptitude for languages bordered on genius. This ability was of great value, living in Europe, and opened up many doors for future stage roles.

His brother Lazarus had always wanted to play Cowboys and Indians, plus anything involving the Wild West and the stories that traveled across the ocean.

He was very excited to move there.

Even so the stress on the family was like a physical assault. It was hardest to understand for the youngest family members. They knew that something was wrong and couldn't understand why the family was crying and so sad.

Their mother was close to a nervous breakdown and, at first, refused to leave. After many days of discussions, she came to realize that they had no choice. Many of their neighbors were close to starvation, and the threat of war seemed constant. At any moment, war could sweep across the European Continent. Every year brought another threat and more bad news.

Chapter 1 Footnotes:

- **Cirque Medrano** started in Toulouse where many famous modern artists got their inspiration for the modern art to come. Everyone fled to Europe when they saw the amazing culture that the circus created in the late 19th century. The Cirque Fernando family had links to the British traveling circus family Robert Austen Brothers. This link led to Cirque Fernando changing its name and becoming a European traveling circus. The name Robert Austen's Mediterranean Circus became Medrano. Medrano was also the name of a Spanish clown employed at the Cirque Fernando in Paris. Past performers have included Buster Keaton together with his wife, Eleanor as a double act between 1947 and 1954, Annie Fratellini, and Arthur Vercoe Pedlar. American actor Billy Beck was the only American to be regularly employed at Medrano as a clown in the early 1950s.

Many years of small wars:
- **War of 1870:** (19 July 1870 – 10 May 1871), was a conflict between the Second French Empire and the German states of the North German Confederation led by the Kingdom of Prussia. The conflict was caused by Prussian ambitions to extend German unification. Some historians argue that the Prussian chancellor Otto. Von Bismarck planned to provoke a French attack to draw the southern German states, Baden, Württemberg, Bavaria and Hesse-Darmstadt, into an alliance with the North German Confederation dominated by Prussia, while others contend that Bismarck did not plan

anything and merely exploited the circumstances as they unfolded.

- **1872 - The Third Carlist War** (Spanish: *Tercera Guerra Carlista*) (1872–1876) was the last Carlist War in Spain. It is very often referred to as the "Second Carlist War", as the 'second' (1847–49) had been small in scale and almost trivial in political consequence. During this conflict, Carlist forces managed to occupy several towns in the interior of Spain, the most important ones being La Seu d'Urgell and Estella in Navarre.Isabella II had abdicated the throne, and Amadeo I, a younger son of the King of Italy who had been proclaimed King of Spain in 1870, was not very popular.

- **1873 - The Cantonal Revolution** was a cantonalist uprising that took place during the First Spanish Republic, starting on July 12 of 1873 in Cartagena. In the following days, it spread through many regions including, Valencia, Andalusia (especially Granada), Cartagena (which endured for several months the besieging army of Nicolás Salmerón) and in the provinces of Salamanca and Ávila, all of them in places that came to articulate cantonalism. It can also be noted, the attempt to establish cantons took place in Extremadura, Coria, Hervás and Plasencia. Pi y Margall, seeing that cantons declared independent by the tardiness of the taxation of improvements, resigned from his post to be succeeded by Salmerón.

Chapter 2
Cirque du Pierre

Uncle Pierre had become an important part of the extended Lézard Family. This fact was especially true for the boys Lorenzo and Lazarus. They spent all their free time with him every chance they got.
Petit Pierre's stories of his many years spent with the traveling circus kept them all talking late into the evenings.
Lorenzo was already fascinated by everything theatrical so the excitement of circus life was all he could think about and soak in.

The First of Many Faces:
Pierre taught him everything he knew about greasepaint, costumes, and performing in front of the crowds of cheering men, women and children.
Both boys spent many hours learning the moves necessary to interact with professional acts such as equestrians, tumblers, rope climbers, high wire walkers, plus changing their persona to become clowns and even the *Carnies who were the backbone of circus and midway life.
This training was an early springboard for Lorenzo's future on the stage and the back alleys of intrigue during the war years. Blending in could be the

difference between life and death. Blending in was also difficult for someone of the Lizard persuasion. His love of languages led him to a joy of reading everything including all the newspapers from all over Europe, no matter what language.

With so many countries nearby he had many neighbors that came from England, Spain, Russia, Germany and even places such as China and Japan. Lorenzo developed a daily neighborhood route where he picked up the papers after his friend's families had finished reading them. They all tried to keep them as pristine as possible because they all liked this inquisitive young boy.

Pierre became even more important to Lorenzo especially after his brother and main sidekick Lazarus was torn away from him. The departure of his mother, father and several siblings was extremely hard on him. Thank God for Pierre, who helped comfort Lorenzo and his two sisters as they adjusted to life with their Aunts and Uncles in Paris.

Over the next few years, many letters steamed back and forth from the family in New York.

It was harder on Lazarus without Lorenzo who was his backup during any diversity. In Europe, there was so much blending of nationalities that there was little prejudice between the races such as humans and lizards however it was much harder in New York. Even with so much more work available the New Yorkers did not like the influx of races from other countries. This prejudice trickled down to school age children, that treated Lazarus as an outsider from the start. He did not have Lorenzo's gift for languages so having to learn English made the rift harder on him. He longed for the day Lorenzo and his siblings would be reunited.

Even though Lorenzo missed his family every day, he still dreaded the day he would have to leave Paris, his beloved City of Light.

Sadly that day was finally approaching. It was a powerful Sweet and Sour emotional roller coaster ride for Lorenzo. The one thing that made it a bit easier was that Pierre was accompanying the three kids. Even with all the travel during his circus days, Pierre had never been to the New World. He had passed letters back and forth with circus people he knew in the States and had been offered a position with the relatively new Ringling Bros. Circus. They wanted to use his European Contacts to bring more acts to their fledgling traveling show.

This boon was great news for Lorenzo and Lazarus alike.

Correspondence and Combat:

Lorenzo had also reached across the ocean to gain

more information and contacts. His drive, at such a young age, was incredible.

To bring his family more income in France, he had spent much of his off time, from school, working for *La Presse, a local newspaper. He did everything from sweeping floors to delivering the papers. Because of his daily habit of reading so many papers, from so many countries, he was able to offer good tips to the journalists. They stopped thinking of him as a kid and asked his advice on stories.

He also liked reading The New York Times, which La Presse saved copies of for him.

One of his early heroes was *Henry Jarvis Raymond, who was the co-founder of the New York Times. Raymond had personally defended his paper's headquarters during the *New York Draft Riots of 1863. He did this by manning a Gatling Gun right in front of his building. This aggressive form of journalism fueled Lorenzo's desire, and drive, to someday become a War

Correspondent. Raymond had also helped President Abraham Lincoln fight the injustice of slavery and prejudice. He used his paper to help Lincoln get elected.

Lorenzo had lived with what prejudice could cause. His brother's letters about what was happening to him in New York fueled a desire to fight it, not with his fists as Lazarus did, but through his writing. He intended to work for the Times in any way possible once he got to New York.

The Footlights of Broadway:

Of course, the theater was extremely important to him as well. He had been in some school plays and through his contacts at La Presse he had scored many free passes to Paris's rollicking entertainment centers. He loved everything from Comedies to Follies, Operettas, Vaudevilles to even Puppet Shows, and more.

He had met and become friends with a large cross-section of entertainers. They loved the energy of the young Lizard, and they all took him under their wings.

This book will be available May 2016

About the Author

Donald G. Parent Jr. is a 100% Disabled Vietnam Veteran. His book "The Warzone PTSD Survivors Guide" has helped veterans all over the world deal with PTSD, TBI, and many other issues.

He teaches veterans the importance of hobbies, art, music, and writing. It is essential to their recovery, from war, to fill their lives with light and joy. As you can see, with this book, he practices what he preaches!

He is married to his best friend of over fifty years - Ginger Parent. They have two daughters and three granddaughters. His oldest granddaughter Hailey also works with the art in this, and other of his books.

Don and Ginger live in the High Desert of Southern California where he loves to commune with the local, friendly, talking lizards to develop ideas for future books and adventures.